Right from the beginning, Abram Noble felt very protective of Martha Lawford.

After a while he left, walking slowly back to the boardinghouse.

"You be sure to bring me your dirty clothes, Mr. Noble," Martha called.

"I will," he yelled back, waving. Before going inside the boardinghouse, he went around back to the corral to make sure his faithful mare, Charity, had plenty of hay and to give her her evening oats. He brushed and curried the rich bay horse. Stroking Charity's darker mane, he felt pride in the shiny plump animal. "I can't wait for you to see her, Charity," her murmured. "I hope you like her as good as I do." After a few more strokes with the brush, he put her in her comfortable stall in the stable and hurried to his own room and bed.

As he lay in bed, he thought about Miss Lawford again. His horse had more to eat and a better place to sleep than the girl and her dog. Somehow that didn't seem right.

But he smiled in the dark, remembering his visit. He had several things to do in the morning. Besides his own donation claim to check out, he had to find out about Miss Lawford's situation. And before he did that he'd better check around to see who needed clothes washed.

"Be with her, God, and protect her. You might be with me, too. I'd be thankin' You a long time if You'd help me get to know her better." He fell into a sound sleep.

VERALEE WIGGINS, author of many books, lives in Washington State with her husband. One of her novels, *Llama Lady*, was voted favorite contemporary inspirational romance by *Heartsong Presents* club members.

Books by VeraLee Wiggins

HEARTSONG PRESENTS

HP17—Llama Lady
HP33—Sweet Shelter
HP76—Heartbreak Trail

Martha My Own

VeraLee Wiggins

A sequel to *Heartbreak Trail*

Heartsong Presents

For Michael and Julie.

May God bless you both forever.

I love you with all my heart,

But He loves you much much more.

ISBN 1-55748-517-8

MARTHA MY OWN

Sporadic tears dampened Martha Ann Lawford's cheeks as she gazed east while leaning against the corner of her covered wagon. The wagon, battered from its long trip west, huddled alone on the north side of a Nez Percé Indian trail.

Immediately before her, eight rough buildings lined the trail, four on each side, forming a sort of dusty street. Behind the buildings on either side, large and small native weeds grew among the drying grass across the prairie. Several dirty light-colored tepees marred the view north of the street, and the three or four shacks on the south did little to improve the view. The few trees in evidence bordered the several rivers and creeks that flowed into and through Steptoeville, Walla Walla Valley, Washington Territory, her new home.

The brilliant sun shining on the snow-capped Blue Mountains forced Martha to shut out the clutter of shacks before her and allowed her to feel better. Surely God had something good planned for her after the long horrible trip she'd just endured.

She shuddered, remembering the terror of crossing those innocent looking hills only ten days ago. They had dragged trees behind the wagons to keep them from careening down the steep hillsides and destroying the wagons and killing the oxen.

I trust You, Lord, but I don't understand why You let our trip west turn into such a disaster. She straightened her shoulders. Keeping her mind and body busy might prevent her from dwelling on the tragedy that had left her alone in a strange place.

"Come on, Josie," she said to her dog, "let's stroll down the street and see what those shacks are." The eight buildings she referred to stood about a hundred feet apart and looked nothing like the fine homes and businesses she'd left in Missouri six long months ago. Some of the buildings were constructed of slab, some of logs. Others consisted of rough boards nailed together in a haphazard fashion. Some had glass windows but most of the windows were made from some translucent material Martha didn't recognize.

Josie, though her ribs and protruding backbone poked almost through her long, matted, black, gray, and white fur, jumped with excitement at the thought of a new adventure.

Martha stepped into the dusty street that snaked under the rickety buildings; there were no sidewalks. A small sign in front of the first building on the north side of the street invited one and all to come in to find warm food and lodging. "They mean people with money," she explained to Josie before noticing her mangy-looking dog tearing up and down the street, raising a large cloud of dust. "Josie!" she called. "You get back here. Now." The dog dropped her tail and scurried back to Martha.

Next they passed a saloon, quickly, for Martha didn't want to be seen near the place. Slowing a few feet past the odious building, she giggled. Who did she think might see her or care what she did in this nearly unpopulated place?

A sign on the next rough wooden building announced it to be a trader's oasis; the roughly painted sign on the small building after that read: Rackett's Tin Shop.

Then she came to a small stream separating the street from a barracks type of place with many buildings. Martha stood at the edge of the creek wondering why the buildings were deserted and what they had been. Then her eyes dropped to the brook before her, gurgling praises to God as it rushed over the smooth rocks. It looked shallow and had two small islands in the middle. After a moment she crossed to the other side of the street to check out the four buildings on the south side: an unoccupied store of some kind, then Chapman and Shaffer's Meat Market, another saloon, and a general store. Two saloons seemed a bit much to Martha considering that the entire town consisted of only these eight shacks.

As she hurried past the second saloon, the front door opened and a wild looking, middle-aged man came pouring out, almost as if propelled by some unseen force, perchance the barkeep's boot? The man gathered himself together, slapped his worn hat back onto his matted gray hair, and started to leave. Then, noticing Martha, he stopped in midstride, a grin splitting his thin lips. His squinty eyes took her in from head to toes.

"Well, whadda we got here?" he asked. "I ain't seen you around, blue eyes. You b'long to someone?"

Suddenly frightened, Martha turned away, but before she could take the first step, his long fingers wound around her arm and jerked her back.

"Why'd a young thing like you walk away when I'm atalkin'?" he asked, his voice thick with alcohol. Before Martha could move, his other arm reached around her and she found her face within inches of the foul-smelling man.'s.

"Josie!" she yelled at the top of her voice, before noticing the dog halfway down the short street, rolling in the dust. "Help, Josie!" she screamed, knowing the man could haul her away before the dog reached her.

Suddenly, the saloon door crashed open again and a taller, younger man emerged almost as quickly as the first man had. "Stop, Abe," the older man hollered as a fist landed somewhere on his person. Raising his hands, he tapped the new arrival's chest in an ineffectual attempt at self-defense. "Stop!" he screamed as a fist slammed into his face. "You ain't got no call to do that." A moment later, Martha's assailant lay in the dust, rubbing the side of his face, a large bruise showing already, and blood running from his mouth.

Finally, Josie arrived barking wildly and growling deep in her throat. Perceiving the man still on his feet to be the enemy, she hit him hard in the chest with her front feet, knocking him backward into the dust beside Martha's would-be assailant. Hopping instantly to his feet, the man dusted off the back of his denim pants. Martha noticed how tall, muscular, and tanned he looked.

In spite of her fear, Martha couldn't hold back a tiny nervous giggle. "No, Josie," she said softly, "you're too late." The dog stood beside her and looked at the men, the fur on her spiny backbone standing erect, a deep growl still rumbling in her throat.

The man who'd administered the beating stood over the downed man. "You'd better get out of here, Slick, before I lose my temper," he said softly. "And if you ever bother a woman again, I'll make you wish you were dead." The tall man had a clean honest look about him but suddenly Martha felt afraid of everyone.

"I didn't mean no harm," the man, Slick, whined. "I was just tryin' to meet the lady." He scrambled to his feet, grabbed his hat again, and lurched off down the street, rubbing his face with one hand and his back with the other.

"Thank you, sir," Martha said, edging away from the

man. If she could get back to her wagon she'd be content to stay there the rest of the day. Maybe forever. What kind of a place had she been dropped into, anyway?

But the man stuck out a big brown paw. "I'm Abram Noble," he said. "Mighty glad to make your acquaintance. Sorry about that fellow. Luckily you won't find many like him around here." He kept the big hand out there forever.

Finally, she allowed him to shake her small hand for a fraction of a second before she withdrew it. "I'm Martha Lawford," she said in a husky voice. "I certainly do thank you, and I'll feel much obliged if there aren't any more around like him."

She turned and started back toward her wagon, only to hear his footsteps behind, then beside her. "Where are you staying, Miss Lawford?" he asked with a familiarity that frightened her all over again. Should she tell him? That wagon with the battered cloth top offered little in the way of protection.

"I'm staying near town," she answered, realizing they'd be at the wagon in minutes. Where could she go to lead him off the track?

He grinned, keeping almost in step with her. "Where near town?" he asked. "I hope you aren't camping alone on the bank of one of the rivers."

She stopped and held a hand to him again. She had to get rid of him now. "No, I'm not. I'm perfectly all right. Thanks for seeing me this far, Mr. Noble. I'll probably see you around town." She turned, lifted her skirt a little, and began striding northwest across the dried grass, away from her wagon, thinking that maybe he'd go back now and she could return to it.

But less than a minute later, he walked beside her again. "I have a bad feelin' about you," he said in an easy, friendly way. "Why don't you just show me where you're staying so I won't worry anymore?"

She liked the man's looks. His clear dark eyes, his thin straight nose, and square jaw, together with his heavy mop of light brown hair gave him an upright, honest, and pleasant looking appearance. She liked his voice, too, and his manner. But he sure knew how to stick—like oatmeal to a pan on an overheated fire. She raised her eyes to meet his and shrugged. "I don't seem to have a choice." She pointed to the covered wagon almost behind them now, and south. "That's my house," she said, turning toward it. They reached it almost immediately. Josie crawled under the wagon into the shade and lay there, watching the pair.

"You can't stay in this thing," Mr. Noble said, stretching his neck to look inside. "It don't offer any protection a'tall. Not from four-legged animals or two." He turned and pointed toward the buildings from which they'd just come. "I'm stayin' at Martin's Boardinghouse. You'd best get a room there, too."

She didn't have to tell him she didn't have money, did she?

After a moment he went on. "What you doing out here alone? Where's your people? And your oxen?"

Martha gave a long loud sigh. She hadn't realized it but she really needed to talk to someone. "Are you purely sure you want to hear?"

"I asked, didn't I?" He sat on the tongue of the wagon. "Let's get comfortable. I have a feeling it's not a pretty story."

"You're right, sir," Martha said, easing down to the makeshift seat. "My older brother, Jackson, got out of the army last year and, ever since, he's talked of nothing else but moving to Walla Walla Valley. Said it was like

the Garden of Eden. He wouldn't stop talking, so finally
our family decided to come. Mama's brother and his wife
and son decided to come, too. We planned to all come
together but my aunt and uncle had a last-minute delay in
collecting the money from their farm. We'd already sold
our place and all our stuff. Everything we owned was in
the wagon so we couldn't wait for them. We'd hoped
they'd catch up with us on the Oregon Trail. They should
be along within a week.

"Our family. . .my parents, two brothers, and I started
west last March with a wagon train from Missouri." She
shook her head, remembering. "It seems a long time ago,
and the trip was so hard." She raised her eyes to his. "I
can't tell you how awful that trip was. But my parents
made it almost here before they. . .," she took a deep breath,
willing herself not to break down in front of this stranger,
"died of cholera." She stopped and dropped her head.
*Why, Lord? I still love You and trust You. . .but why did
they have to die? I loved them so much. And needed them
desperately.* Raising her head resolutely, she continued.
"We ran out of food right after that and my oxen were so
worn-out we had to leave them at Fort Hall.

"One of the families had extra oxen so they pulled me
this far. They wanted me to go on with them but I have to
wait here for my aunt and uncle." Her eyes burned so she
shut them tight. "I have to wait for them, Mr. Noble," she
continued a moment later. "They're all the family I have
left. Finally, the Butler family gave me some flour and
left me here, but they took my baby brother, William.
Said I'd have all I could do to take care of myself until
my aunt and uncle come. We'll get him next summer."

Swallowing loudly, Martha closed her eyes tightly
again. She'd never felt so alone in her entire life. If
Josie would just come out from under the wagon, she'd

give her a big hug.

Martha straightened her shoulders and smiled at the man, Mr. Noble. When she met his gaze, his red-rimmed eyes looked almost ready to cry, too.

His Adam's apple jerked up and down. "I guess that's about what I expected. What about your other brother? He die, too?"

She shook her dark head. "When we left the oxen at Fort Hall, he decided to go back and make sure our aunt and uncle were all right." She shook her head again. "I wish he hadn't. I need him more than they do."

They sat together in silence, each deep in private thoughts. She wondered why she'd told this stranger all her troubles. Now he knew her total vulnerability.

Finally, he met her gaze. "You don't have any money, right?"

She nodded. "But I can work. Maybe I could work at the boardinghouse. I know how to clean, and I can cook a little."

He dropped his eyes. "That's another sad story. The man got hurt bad so his wife and four daughters run the place. I think they're pretty broke." He leaned forward, his elbows on his knees, his chin in his hands, thinking. "You don't happen to play the piano, do you?"

She laughed out loud. As if anyone in this little town would pay her for playing. "As a matter of fact, I do," she said. "Is someone at the boardinghouse looking for a pianist?"

He shook his light brown head. "No. But there are two saloons. I'll bet I could talk one of them into hiring you. You could wait tables when you aren't playing."

"Sorry, I don't set foot into saloons, Mr. Noble. Don't you know they're the devil's playground?"

two

Abram Noble enjoyed the feel of the cold water on his face and arms as he washed up for supper; it really brought a man to life. But he kept thinking of the girl at the covered wagon.

He continued thinking of her as he ate the steaming meal Mrs. Martin and her daughters had prepared. Potatoes fried with onions in bacon grease, boiled turnips, some kind of meat. Roast horse, he thought to himself, trying to chew it. Boiled cabbage, tea, and bread and butter finished out the meal. He'd been there only three days but twice they'd served various kinds of melons. He'd enjoyed that all right.

He hardly heard the other men laughing and talking about how the strange girl had affected his brain. True, he could hardly force his thoughts from her.

In his mind he saw her long dark hair braided into a crown too heavy for her nicely shaped head. Enormous bright blue eyes shone from her heart-shaped face with its ivory complexion. Average height, but small boned, she looked young, very young. All together, she made a picture that Abe couldn't get out of his mind for even five minutes. Too bad her dress and sunbonnet were so worn and faded; they were not the proper clothes for a girl like Miss Lawford.

What would become of her? He'd gladly rent a room for her but he could tell from their encounter that she'd never accept help. No telling what could happen to her out there alone.

When he finished supper, his feet hit the dusty path. Clearly visible from the boardinghouse, the wagon sat on the north side of the trail only about a hundred yards west.

Nearing the wagon he noticed the girl had a small fire going and some kind of pot over the low flames. "Hello, Miss Lawford," he called in order not to startle her with his sudden appearance. "Thought I'd better make sure you're all right before—"

Josie the dog interrupted, bursting from beneath the wagon and with the roar of a tornado. Abe, remembering his earlier encounter with the animal, jumped back and forgot what he'd intended to say and almost about Miss Lawford altogether.

"Josie, girl! Stop!" the young woman commanded. The dog quieted immediately but planted herself between Abe and her mistress.

Abe felt a letdown. Why couldn't the dog have slept through his visit?

The girl returned her attention to the pot on the fire. It looked like white dough in the bottom, almost like a pancake but not quite. She scraped the stuff from the bottom, turned it over, and took the pot off the fire.

She smiled at him. "I'd offer you a chair if I had one." Then she brightened. "I have two boxes that I can empty real easy and we can sit on them." She jumped up from her position beside the fire where she'd been sitting on her heels. "I'll be right back," she said, hopping lightly to the frame of the wagon and disappearing under its white canopy. She appeared a moment later and dropped the boxes gently to the ground, before jumping down behind them. "Sit down and relax, Mr. Noble. These are dynamite boxes we packed food in."

She returned the pot to the fire. "I have to finish cooking our supper because I don't have many buffalo chips left. When it's finished, I can talk for a while." As Abe watched, she poured another batch of the pasty stuff into the pot and watched it carefully until she scraped it loose from the bottom and turned it over. A few minutes later she took it out of the pot and put more in. Then she cooked two more from the remaining paste.

"There," she said, plopping onto one of the boxes. "We can eat later. It won't matter if they're cold."

"Would you mind telling me what you just cooked?" Abe asked.

Miss Lawford smiled and dipped her head a bit. "Why, Mr. Noble, haven't you seen trail bread? I make it from flour and water." She shrugged. "It's supposed to have other things in it but flour's all we have." Josie whined and tried to snoot Miss Lawford's hand toward the bread. The dog's pitiful cries made Abe's heart ache for the half-starved animal.

The frail girl shrugged and fed one of the breads to the dog who took it in one gulp. "Sorry," she said. "We each get only a couple of these twice a day and you can see Josie's eager."

"Is that all you got to eat?"

Miss Lawford nodded, her face turning an attractive pink. "We're mighty thankful to have that, Mr. Noble. Our food was completely gone. No one on the wagon train had much either, but they gave me enough flour to last a week. . .until my aunt and uncle come."

Abe felt almost sick to think of this lovely girl trying to care for herself and her dog. And both of them nearly starving. "I got a gun," he said. "I could get you some meat. Rabbits, or something."

She perked up a moment, then settled down. "Only if you have too much for yourself," she said. "I have a gun too, but I'm afraid to shoot it." Josie put her front feet into Miss Lawford's lap, who then got up and fed Josie another piece of trail bread. It disappeared pitifully fast. Then she gave the dog one more, leaving only one small piece.

"I have a plan," she told Abe, her delicate face showing excitement. "Why couldn't I do washing for the men in the boardinghouse? Or wherever they live. I could do it right on the banks of that little creek down past the buildings." She pointed east, down the street. "How are people getting their things washed now?"

Abe, only in town three days himself, hadn't given that problem a thought yet. He shook his head. "I'm not sure, but I'll find out. That would be hard work."

Her laugh sounded like birds singing. "I'm not afraid of hard work, Mr. Noble. I washed clothes for several of the people in the wagon train. I spent most of my Saturday afternoons washing clothes. It wasn't easy but it was something I could do to help. One person was sick, one old and weak, some didn't even have wagons." She sighed then pulled her shoulders back. "My only problem right now is that I don't have any tallow to make soap."

He laughed. "I can buy you some soap right there in that first building on the right. It's a general store and sells most anything a man needs."

She stiffened. "I couldn't let you do that, Mr. Noble. Josie and I aren't your responsibility."

That idea didn't sound half bad to Abe. Never had he met anyone who made him feel so responsible. But he had to be careful not to frighten her away. "Maybe I could loan you the soap and you could repay me or do some of my clothes for free. Would that work?"

"Yes. It sounds good. Thank you, Mr. Noble. You really are, aren't you?"

"I really am what?"

"Noble." They laughed together. When they finished, she cast a questioning glance his way. "You know all about me but I know nothing about you, sir. That hardly seems fair."

She wanted to know about him? She'd opened up enough to ask? Well, he'd best not keep the lady waiting! "I hail from Iowa and have two parents and two sisters. I been in the army for the last six years. Got sent west to fight the Indians and that's what I been doing. Me and my company chased some Indian tribes past here a couple times and I noticed what a right purty valley it was. I sure understand how your brother felt.

"I tried to file a donation claim several years ago but they weren't allowing settlers in yet because of the Indian wars. No matter where I went, I kept remembering this little valley where the rivers meet. Well, finally the army turned me loose and the government opened the valley to settlers, so here I am. I'm looking for a piece of land I can't live without, so I can put a claim on it."

A look of pure bliss crossed Miss Lawford's face. "That's exactly what I'd like to do, too," she said.

At first Abe felt excitement at the possibility of having her for a neighbor. Then he remembered a man had to be twenty-one years old to make a claim. This slip of a girl couldn't be a day over fifteen. He wasn't sure whether women could make claims, anyway. "How old are you?" he asked quietly.

"I'm seventeen," she replied. "How old are you, sir?"

He laughed. After all, fair was fair. "I'm an old man,"

he said. "I'll celebrate my twenty-fifth birthday in December."

She nodded. "And what do you plan to do with this claim you're getting?"

He thought a moment. "Well, farm it, I guess, and run some cattle. Maybe some sheep and a few chickens. Plant me some fruit trees. I guess that ought to about do it."

"Oh, Mr. Noble, it sounds heavenly. I'm going to do it, too. First, I have to earn some money washing clothes to buy food for Josie and me, then I'm going to get a donation claim, too. I really am."

As dusk began to drop her curtain over them, Abe noticed mosquitoes. "I hope you will, Miss Lawford, but for now, how about letting me lend you enough money to get a room in the boardinghouse? I don't want you out here. You got no protection a'tall."

A smile curved her lips. "What do you call the hurricane that met you, Mr. Noble? Josie would die to protect me. I'd better stay right here until my aunt and uncle come. It may not be a palace, but it's free."

"You heard about the Indians?"

Her face blanched and her right hand flew to her throat. "What about the Indians?"

He smiled. "I never heard about them hurting anyone, but they walk right into people's houses and demand food. Everyone I know's given them something to eat and they leave. They stink like nothing you've ever smelled because they smear fish fat all over them. They think it keeps 'em warm. They scare people a lot, but as far as I know they don't hurt anyone."

"Oh, but I don't have anything to feed them. I'm nearly out of flour, too. That's why I have to wash clothes."

He smiled grimly. "You'll give them something to eat,

Miss Lawford, even if it's your last bite." Seeing her dismay he tried to think of something with which to cheer her. "They probably won't come here anyway, seeing you don't have a proper house."

"I hope not. I really hope not, Mr. Noble. That would purely frighten me to death."

After a little while he left, walking slowly back to the boardinghouse.

"You be sure to bring me your dirty clothes, Mr. Noble," Martha called.

"I will," he yelled back, waving. Before going inside the boardinghouse, he went around back to the corral to make sure his faithful mare, Charity, had plenty of hay and to give her her evening oats. He brushed and curried the rich bay horse. Stroking Charity's darker mane, he felt pride in the shiny plump animal. "I can't wait for you to see her, Charity," he murmured. "I hope you like her as good as I do." After a few more strokes with the brush, he put her in her comfortable stall in the stable and hurried to his own room and bed.

As he lay in bed, he thought about Miss Lawford again. His horse had more to eat and a better place to sleep than the girl and her dog. Somehow that didn't seem right.

But he smiled in the dark, remembering his visit. He had several things to do in the morning. Besides his own donation claim to check out, he had to find out about Miss Lawford's situation. And before he did that he'd better check around to see who needed clothes washed.

"Be with her, God, and protect her. You might be with me, too. I'd be thankin' You a long time if You'd help me get to know her better." He fell into a sound sleep.

three

Martha watched Mr. Noble striding away from her wagon until he went around the boardinghouse and was out of sight. "Well," she told Josie. "I think he'll really help me get started washing clothes. Maybe I'll make enough to buy you all the food you need." She hugged the dog's big head. Josie returned the caress with two swipes of her tongue across Martha's cheek. "Just you wait," Martha continued. "Things'll soon be better. I promise." She turned to the cold trail bread. Knowing she needed the strength the bread offered, she had a hard time getting out her next words. "We'll start right now. I already gave you three of the breads, but you're still hungrier than I. Here, you can have half of this last one." The dog didn't wait for a second invitation but gobbled the offered food.

Martha sat back down on the box and tried to make her piece last as long as possible. She chewed each tiny bite thirty-two times as her mother had taught her, and tried to think about something besides the food. The only other thing she could think about was the washing she might have to do and the strength she would need to do it. She took another tiny bite. As she chewed, three men approached the wagon from the west. Where had they come from? The street and people were the other way. Even the tepees were east and north. Becoming uneasy, she wondered who they could be and what they wanted.

Then she recognized Indians! She sat with her heart in her throat, terrified. *Protect me, Father. Make them be friendly.* When a deep growl rumbled from inside Josie, she reached an arm around her faithful dog's neck.

They stopped within ten feet of Martha, stared into her eyes, and waited. An almost unbearable stench, arriving with the Indians, made Martha's stomach lurch. She didn't know what to say or do. Would they even understand her language?

The three walked over to the tiny fire, and looked into the empty pot. One of them began motions as if eating. "Food," he said. He seemed to be the oldest of the three and wore buckskins. Soft moccasins covered his feet. The other two wore white man's clothes, worn and dirty overalls with ragged long-sleeved shirts. But like the older man, they wore soft deerskin moccasins. Long, matted black hair hung down their backs.

The old Indian caught her attention again, then repeated his request for food. Or was it an order?

Mr. Noble had warned her they'd want food. But she had so little! What would she do when it was gone?

"Food!" the Indian said again. The three surrounded her as she sat on the box and Josie's rumble grew louder. Mr. Noble had told her to feed them even if it was her last bite.

"You be good, Josie," she warned the dog. Scrambling to her feet, her knees shaking, she tossed four more buffalo chips onto the fire, poured two cups of her precious flour into the bowl and added water. When thoroughly mixed, she dropped spoonfuls onto the bottom of the pot.

The Indians looked friendlier as they watched her fixing the trail bread. They said something to each other then they all sat down beside the box she'd abandoned.

After turning the bread twice, she scooped it from the pot, cooled it a moment, and handed each Indian a piece.

They nodded deeply, saying something unintelligible. "You're welcome," she said, smiling. This wasn't nearly as bad as she'd feared—except she could ill afford losing the flour.

As each man took a bite, his expression changed to surprise then anger. All three jumped to their feet and started saying something to Martha at the same time. It didn't take her long to decide they didn't like the trail bread and wanted something else—now!

"I don't have anything else," she said, knowing they wouldn't understand her. "That's all my dog and I have to eat," she went on.

They caught the word "dog" and one of them gestured toward Josie, making motions of eating again. Martha dropped to her knees, reaching her arms around her friend. "No, no," she said. She kissed Josie's dusty face. "I love my dog. I'd never eat her."

After a few moments of talking together, the Indians tossed the trail bread to Josie, who wolfed it down. Then they left without another word. Martha watched them, wondering to which tepee they'd go, but soon they became specks on the western horizon. She dropped to the box, breathing hard.

She started laughing with relief, then couldn't stop. Realizing she'd become hysterical, she forced herself to take deep breaths until she regained control. Then she thought about their rejection of her food and used all her willpower not to start laughing again. "Well, Josie, at least they won't be back to bother us anymore. That's something, isn't it?" Their terrible stink still lingered heavily in the air so she took Josie for a walk down the street to the creek. After her meeting with the Indians, the buildings with people in them seemed to offer a modicum of protection.

A half-hour later she returned to find the air around the wagon fresh again so she washed the pot and bowl. She lay down in her wagon bed and thanked God for making the Indians friendly. "Thank You for my new friend, Mr. Noble. Protect me from everyone and everything and help me get along without my parents." She hesitated as a few tears rolled down her cheeks. "Help me not to miss baby William so much. I know he's better off with Rachel and her mama and papa, but I miss him. I love You, God. Good night." She hardly noticed the growling of her stomach and tried not to think about the wasted food. Well, the food wasn't wasted. Maybe Josie's backbone wouldn't stick out quite so far now. Tomorrow would be a better day. She fell asleep listening to mosquitoes buzzing around her head.

இ

Martha wakened early the next morning, feeling the warm sun shining through the white wagon top. She tried hard not to think about the Indians. Thinking how different it would be if her folks were here, she reminded herself that they'd want her to get up and get going.

After carrying back the second bucket of water from the creek (she'd bathed with the first one), she mixed up a batch of trail bread. Josie stood beside her, watching every move she made until movement from the street attracted her attention. She exploded into excited barks.

"Good morning, Miss Lawford," Mr. Noble said. "I have a fresh rabbit for you. Am I too late?"

Martha's stomach made an extra loud growl, and Josie showed intense interest in the dressed animal hanging from the man's hand. "Oh, thank you, Mr. Noble, sir," she said, reaching for it. She wasted no time before washing it, cutting it into pieces, and dropping it into a kettle of water. "This certainly will be a treat," she said. "I thank you more than you know, sir." Josie whined and her sad eyes met Martha's. "Would you mind if I share it with Josie?" Martha asked hesitantly.

"I'd be disappointed if you didn't."

Martha wondered if she should invite Mr. Noble to eat, too, but that would be getting far too familiar at this point. He seemed to be a nice man all right, but she mustn't encourage any man's friendship right now. What did she know about men?

"I'll be back in a while," the man said, interrupting her thoughts. "I'll go see if I can find anyone who needs some washing done. I'll bring back a bar of soap, too."

Martha and Josie each had two pieces of trail bread while they waited for the savory smelling rabbit to finish cooking. "We're going to be so stuffed we won't be able to walk to the creek," she told her dog. But they had no trouble eating the entire rabbit. After they finished, Martha sat on her wooden box, thinking. Not all that long ago she'd have insisted her rabbit be rolled in flour or cornmeal and fried in deep fat with lots of salt. But never had anything, including rabbit, tasted better than this one, boiled in water with nothing else. She had a feeling that Josie, who had eaten two-thirds of the fresh meat, could have had even more.

Well, she might as well try to figure a way to wash clothes. "Come on, Josie," she called, heading east toward the creek. She arrived in five minutes having met not a soul on the walk.

She walked down to the water and squatted. Maybe she could dig a hole in the shallow water by removing rocks. Grabbing stones by the handful, she tossed them downstream. Soon, she had a deep enough spot to dip from or to soak clothes in. She'd roiled the water, but it would soon settle back down.

She looked around. Not a single twig or branch with which to make a fire. If there had ever been any, someone had beaten her to them. She couldn't use her buffalo chips. They were almost gone, too, and she'd never get any more of them. Sitting on the rocks on the creek bank, Martha enjoyed the warm sun on her back. She looked around again. At least she could dry the clothes on the small bushes scattered along the bank. Maybe she could soak the clothes overnight with lots of soap, then wash them in cold water.

"Come, Josie," she called, gathering up her skirt. Maybe she could beat the dog back to the wagon if she really raced. She took off.

Laughing over her shoulder at her surprised dog, Martha nearly ran into a girl about her own age. The girl's frightened shout stopped Martha within touching distance. Martha stepped back a few feet and gazed into the girl's blazing blue eyes. Much shorter then Martha, she looked nice enough, but her round face expressed indignation at being nearly run down directly in front of the boarding-house—her own home. The girl wore a coarse gown of an indescribable color, maybe light brownish gray, and a matching sunbonnet. Her eyes looked as though they'd burst into flame any minute. She looked up and down the street then back at Martha.

"What were you running from?" she finally demanded.

Martha laughed. "Nothing. I just felt like racing with my dog."

The girl stared at Martha, as though trying to figure her out. "Who are you? Where are you staying?"

Remembering her manners, Martha extended her hand to the girl. "I'm Martha Lawford, and I'm really not staying anywhere yet. My aunt and uncle will be coming on the next wagon train. I guess I'll just stay in my wagon until they get here." As she explained she pointed west to her wagon, its dirty white top contrasting boldly against the deep blue sky and the nearly dried grass in the foreground.

The girl's mouth turned into a round *O*. "You're the one Mr. Noble was telling us about. Well, I'm Nellie Martin. Mama and us girls do the boarders' washing. Ain't many other people 'round."

Martha's mouth went dry. "What about the people who run the stores?" she asked. "Do they all live here?"

Nellie nodded her red head. "Most of our boarders own or work at the trading post. We do their washing. A lot of the others live in the back of their stores. They ain't married, and I don't know how they git their washin' done."

At that news Martha felt life flow through her body again. She'd have plenty of people to wash for—if she could just get the clothes clean. "How long have you been here?" she asked. "Do you like it?"

Nellie gazed off toward the Blue Mountains, her fingers curving as she mentally counted. "About eight months," she finally said. "That's when settlers were first allowed in. Mama wanted to own the first boardinghouse. We all worked in a boardinghouse in The Dalles after Papa got his leg smashed off cutting logs. Mama said she could do better than Mrs. Adamson, so we came."

Martha needed to get started washing clothes, but it had been several days since she'd seen another girl. She hoped Nellie would become her friend.

"Come in and meet Mama and my sisters," Nellie said.

"She'd tan my hide if I didn't bring you in. There's only one other woman in the village that I know about."

"Oh, you look so young," Mrs. Martin said. "I hear you've been left all alone in the world. Can I do anything for you, my dear?"

"Would you have work I could do? I know how to clean and I can cook simple food."

A sad look crossed the woman's face. "I'd like to, but we barely get enough money from the men to buy food. One of these days things will be different. But if you don't have anything to eat, you just come eat with us. We eat breakfast at six o'clock, dinner at twelve sharp, and supper at six o'clock in the evening. You just come any time, hon."

Martha didn't refuse but she knew she'd have to be *really* hungry to take advantage of the woman's kind offer. Besides, what about Josie? She couldn't eat somewhere and forget her best friend. She almost smiled thinking what Mrs. Martin would say if she asked for food for her dog.

After a few more minutes, Martha managed to get away and ran back to the wagon where Josie waited in the shade. The sun stood almost overhead and Martha felt hungry, but she couldn't think of food until evening. She'd just gather up her tubs and carry them down to the creek. Maybe someone would see what she was doing and offer her some work. If not, she could wash her own things. As she hurried around, Josie announced the arrival of Mr. Noble.

He carried a bunch of clothes, a long-sleeved shirt on the outside with the sleeves and tails tied together to form a bundle. "I found some work for you," he said. Then he pulled a large yellow bar from his back pocket. "Soap, too." His grin looked completely satisfied. "I see you're getting ready. Come on. I'll help you carry the things over to the creek."

"Oh, I can do that, Mr. Noble. It won't matter if I make several trips. I have nothing else to do, anyway." She hopped up into the wagon. "I think I have some paper in here," she called. "I'll just write down the price of the soap." A moment later she jumped lightly to the ground, a piece of dirty, torn paper and a stub of a pencil in her hand. She looked expectantly at Mr. Noble. He grinned. "Well, how much is the soap?" she asked.

"Fifty cents. Is that too much?"

She laughed. "Whatever you paid is the price, Mr. Noble. I won't complain." She wrote **Expenses** at the top and under that she added: *Soap—$.50.*

"Now I feel like a businesswoman," she said, shoving the paper and pencil under the edge of the wagon canopy. Picking up two nested tubs, she started off. Mr. Noble grabbed the clothes and the large bucket, and followed her. "Don't worry about the money, Mr. Noble," she said as they hurried down the street. "I'll pay you as soon as I can."

"Forget the money," he said. "I thought you agreed to wash my clothes in exchange for the soap."

When they both had dropped their burdens on the clean stones beside the creek, they sat with their backs to the sun. "How you going to heat the water?" he asked.

She shook her head. "I couldn't find anything to make a fire. Think I could soak them overnight in lots of soap and wash them tomorrow in cold water?"

A smile tugged at the left side of his mouth before he shrugged. "I've never washed clothes. You wash them and I'll take them back."

Deciding she might as well get the clothes soaking, she rubbed the bar of soap vigorously, trying to make some suds. A few bubbles floated to the top so she continued rubbing until her arms gave out. Puffing, she sat down in the warm sun to rest.

Mr. Noble reached for the soap bar. "Here, let me help with that," he said with a smile. "I'll bet I can work up some suds." Before Martha could object, he grabbed the bar and worked it over. He looked at her, puffing and laughing. "How's that? Think it's ready for the clothes?"

She untied the shirt sleeves and started lifting the clothes into the water. Whew! The stink made her glad they were outdoors. And glad she'd forgotten to bring her own things. She dropped in two pairs of heavy overalls, so filthy they felt stiff, one of which someone had obviously wiped his hand on after blowing his nose onto the ground. She'd never put her clothes into the same water with this filth! She wasn't sure she could put her hands into it. Then she shoved in two unwieldy and equally filthy shirts, followed by a pair of badly stained and malodorous long johns. After she had all the clothes shoved into the water, she pushed them around and around, up and down. She hadn't thought about how seldom these men's clothes got washed. Or what a miserable job it would be. How would she ever get the clothes clean again? Or her hands? If she could find a stout stick she could use that to shove the things around. But there wasn't one stick of any kind anywhere.

Mr. Noble struggled to his feet. "I'll go on back," he said. "I guess you'll leave these things here tonight?"

She nodded, holding her filthy hands away from her body. "They'll be safe, won't they?"

He laughed out loud. "If anyone started taking those

grimy clothes, he'd think again. I've never seen anything safer than that stuff." He gave her a salute and headed west toward the boardinghouse.

She sat enjoying the warm sun for a while, then shoved the clothes around again. The cold water seemed to be doing something. At least it looked almost black. Maybe she should dump it and get clean water. "Thank You, God for helping me get the clothes to wash. I'm sorry I acted like a baby, but I'm purely thankful for having clothes to wash. I love You, Father." Before she added the "amen," she heard a man shouting and cursing. Then Josie appeared, sliding down the creek bank with something bloody in her mouth.

Slick, the man who'd attacked Martha that first day, appeared a moment later with a thick stick in his hand. "Get that dog," he yelled. "It stole my meat and I'm killin' it." Josie splashed across the creek and tore off through the grass, the man following at a much slower pace. About the time Slick stepped from the water onto the other side, his boots dripping, Josie dashed back across to Martha where she then stopped to shake off her excess water. Martha snatched the bloody meat from Josie's mouth. "No!" she said. "Bad dog!" She pointed down the street to the wagon. "Go home, Josie," she commanded. "Go!" The dog took off, looking much less exuberant than she had with the meat in her mouth. Martha wanted nothing more than to give it back to her skinny dog, but she had to make peace somehow.

She met Slick as he stepped from the water. "Here's your meat," she said. "Not even hurt."

He looked at her in surprise, then slapped the meat from her hand to the ground. "You! I shoulda knowed you'd be back causin' more trouble. Well, I ain't eatin' after no dog. Pay for the meat or I'll kill the dog. Take yer pick, girlie."

Martha knew she was dealing with a dangerous man. And for all she knew he might be quoting the law of the land out here in the wild country. "I'll wash your clothes free, Mr. . . .uh. . .I'll do more than enough to pay for your meat."

"Whadda I want my clothes washed fer? Ain't no wimmin out here no how. Just gimme the money and I'll go back to the meat shop."

Not having any money and not knowing what to say, she bent over the tub of dirty clothes and stirred them around.

"Ya ain't got no money, have ya?" he yelled at her. "I know ya ain't." He looked around. "Where'd that dog go, anyway? I'm goin' after the thievin' mutt right now." He bumbled unsteadily off down the street, as if he might have been at the saloon before the meat market.

four

Abe Noble cleaned himself up a little, then decided to go see what was happening at the saloon. Stepping through the front door of the boardinghouse to the dusty street, he heard a rough voice yelling. Sounded like Slick. Remembering Miss Lawford at the creek, he sprinted in that direction. As he neared, Slick lurched off across the street toward Galbraith's Saloon. Abe slowed to a fast walk and continued to the creek.

Miss Lawford leaned over her tub with her back to him. "What's wrong with Slick?" Abe called.

When the girl turned around, she brushed a tear off her face, then quickly faced the tub again, jerking the clothes around.

He stepped down beside her. "Slick been bothering you again?" he asked, fearing to hear the answer. She remained silent. "What did Slick do?" he asked louder than necessary.

He heard a tiny sniff. She jammed the clothes up and down. Then, "Nothing, yet. He's going to kill Josie."

Then he noticed the meat lying on the ground. "Where'd this come from?" he asked, turning it over with the toe of his boot.

Miss Lawford kept stirring the clothes in the black water. She hiccuped loudly, then drew in a deep breath. "Josie took it from Mr. . . .uh. . .Slick."

"Why didn't you give it back?"

Another hiccup. "He. . .he. . .doesn't like eating after

a dog."

Abe began laughing. He couldn't help it. Easing himself down to the warm rocks, his back to the sun, he laughed some more.

Finally, Miss Lawford turned to face him. "It isn't funny, sir. My dog didn't mean to do anything wrong. She's been hungry for so long she'd eat anything she could get."

Abe made a determined effort to calm his hilarity. When he had himself under control, he moved to her side. "I know. It just struck my funny bone to think of that old coot eating after a dog." He chuckled again, then managed to stop. "Josie should be the one who wouldn't eat after him, wouldn't you think?" he asked, still grinning.

"I don't know, sir. But I can't let him hurt Josie."

He nodded. "Right. I'll go have me a little talk with Slick. He won't hurt your dog, Miss Lawford. Don't you worry." He almost flinched, watching her soft hands reaching into that grimy water. "Want me to help you get fresh water before I go talk to Slick?" he asked. "I'll make more suds for you, too."

She shook her head. "I can do it, Mr. Noble. Please go tell that man he can't hurt Josie. Please?"

"But I hate to see you working so hard." He took her other tub, filled it with water, then spun the soap bar between his hands until he worked up some suds. He smiled at the appreciation showing in her bright blue eyes. "I'd offer to transfer those dirty clothes but I know you wouldn't let me. So I'm off to talk to the town drunk." He walked a little way before a thought struck him. "Be sure to take that meat home for Josie," he called. Then he strode off to Chapman and Shaffer's Meat Market.

"Seen Slick lately?" he asked.

"Yeah," Will Shaffer growled, "he stoled one of my best roasts about an hour ago."

Abe burst into laughter again. He couldn't remember when his life had been so riotous. "I could return that roast if you want it," he said. He pointed toward the creek. "It's lying out there on the creek bank, quite a lot worse for wear." Then he told the man how Slick had lost the roast and threatened Miss Lawford's dog.

"You just tell the young woman to let her dog have it," Shaffer said. "How was that rabbit you bought this morning? Tough?"

Abe shook his head. "Just fine, Will. Never ate better in my life. You got another one?"

"I got a couple. Want one?"

"Yeah, I'll take 'em both." Abe took the rabbits, wrapped in rough brown paper, and headed toward Galbraith's Saloon. Stepping inside, he waved to a couple of men, then, not seeing Slick, crossed the street to Ball and Stone. He hadn't been in that saloon before but it seemed a likely place to find the man he sought. Slick sat at the bar not far from the door. Abe slid onto the stool beside the smaller man.

"What'll it be?" the barkeep asked.

"How about a bacon sandwich?" Abe asked.

"Comin' up."

Abe turned to Slick. "Heard you lost a little meat this afternoon."

"Yeah! I'm gonna git that dog. Show that high falutin' dame, too."

Abe shoved one of the rabbits down the bar to Slick. "You aren't going to do one thing to that dog, Slick. Remember what happened the other day when you bothered Miss Lawford? Well, that'll seem like a Sunday school picnic compared to what I'll do to you if you so much as touch either her or her dog. Don't push me, Slick. Sometimes I go off like a loaded gun."

Taking his newly arrived bacon sandwich, he hopped off the stool, grabbed the remaining rabbit, and headed for the door. "I hear the city's takin' stiffer measures against thieves, Slick. Better watch it."

"Haw!" Slick snorted. "The way I hear it the town's brand new police force, Sheriff Jackson, ain't even got a gun. Who's doin' all this stiffer measure stuff?"

Abe stepped out of the saloon and drew a deep breath of fresh air. Looking east and not seeing Miss Lawford, he turned west. He dropped the brown paper from the rabbit, making a mental note to pick it up on his way back. Miss Lawford would never accept the rabbit if it came in brown paper. That would smack of charity. Maybe he'd get the rabbit there in time to save her precious trail bread. That stuff didn't look too good, but it must be edible.

As he neared the covered wagon, a small spiral of smoke cut into the blue sky. Then the dog burst from beneath the wagon and came after him as if he were the devil in disguise. Miss Lawford called Josie back.

"Good evening," Abe called when he could be heard. Then he held out the rabbit. "I got lucky again," he said. "This may be the last one in the county though." He hadn't lied, he told himself proudly. He had gotten lucky and it might be the last one for all he knew.

She accepted the rabbit graciously with profuse thanks. "You surely didn't need to dress it out for me, Mr. Noble. That's one thing I learned on the Trail."

When she turned those blue eyes on him, he felt himself melting like bacon grease in the hot sun. He didn't mention it to Miss Lawford, but he'd have shaved that rabbit, hair by hair, and cut it into bite-sized pieces if he thought it would please her.

She washed the rabbit, cut it up, and dropped it into a

kettle of water as she had this morning. "Won't you sit down, Mr. Noble?" she invited after he stood for a few minutes.

After they rested a moment she turned worried eyes to him. "Is that awful man going to hurt Josie?"

He shook his head. "I guarantee he won't hurt you or your dog, Miss Lawford. I just wish I could be sure about every other man in the county."

They visited a while, she telling him about the Indians' visit.

"You mean they just walked off without eating?" he asked.

She giggled. "That's what they did. At first they didn't like it but they soon decided they'd rather have no food than trail bread. They won't bother me again, do you think?"

Abe didn't feel all that sure about the Indians. He didn't know much about them, except they stank and walked into people's houses, expecting to be fed. Everyone he'd known had fed them. He shook his head. "I don't know."

She smiled. "I think they've had more than enough of me. Oh yes, I met Nellie Martin, too." She went on to tell how she almost ran over the girl in her race with Josie. "I hope she'll be my friend. Being all alone, I purely need a friend."

"I'm sure she needs one, too," he said. Then he told how Slick appropriated the meat Josie took from him. "You gave it back to her, didn't you?" he asked.

She nodded. "I did because she's so terribly thin. I hope it won't encourage her to do something like that again."

"It won't." Abe couldn't help noticing how thin Miss Lawford appeared to be, too. Her worn blue dress hung loosely, even at the waist. Then he remembered something. "I checked into the donation claims today."

Miss Lawford sprang from her box. Then she sat down again, but with excitement in her eyes and voice. "How many acres can you get? Can a woman get a claim, too? Tell me about it, Mr. Noble. I purely want one of those donation claims."

"Well, the news isn't all good. The claim for a single person is one hundred sixty acres, for a married couple, three hundred twenty. Yes, a woman can make a claim but a ma. . .anyone must be twenty-one unless they're married to someone who is."

Miss Lawford looked crushed for a moment, then relaxed. "I'll just have to stay with my uncle until I'm old enough," she said with resignation. "But you just wait, Mr. Noble. I'm having a farm of my own."

Abe smiled. "I believe you Miss Lawford. I just wish you could get started right away." *But what if they're all taken before you turn twenty-one?* he thought. Four years is a long time. Wisely, he said nothing to discourage her.

&

When Abe finally got into bed that night, Miss Lawford's bright eyes, sensitive mouth, dark hair, and thin body kept watching him while he tried to fall asleep.

"Lord," he said aloud. "You watch over that little girl, hear? I worry about her out there alone." He grinned. "But then You care a whole lot more for her than I do, don't You? I guess I can trust You to watch over her. I'll watch over her all I can, too, God."

He'd never in his life seen such a lovely unspoiled girl. What he'd give to have her on the next farm beside his. What he'd give to have her on his own farm! He finally fell asleep but Miss Lawford invaded even his dreams.

five

Martha shared the rabbit with Josie, even after the dog had eaten Slick's entire roast. Due to Mr. Noble's lengthy visit, the rabbit had cooked so long it nearly fell off the bones. Martha didn't care, neither did Josie. In fact the dog chewed the softened bones and swallowed them.

After supper Martha and Josie sprinted down the dusty street to the creek where Martha gave the dirty clothes a hundred pushes, shoves, and stirs. The water looked as black as it had before Mr. Noble had changed it but she felt far too tired to get clean water again. Walking back to the wagon, she decided to get up early in the morning so she could finish the clothes and they could start drying.

Was this to be her life from now on? She hadn't realized how distasteful the work would be, but who was she, who needed the work so desperately, to complain? What would she do when the weather cooled? Well, she'd just thank the Lord for letting her do it until Aunt Mandy and Uncle Cleve came. They'd never think of letting her do such awful work after they got here anyway. *Bless them, Lord, as they travel. Keep them safe and hurry their steps. Bless Jackson, too, and William.* Her breath came evenly and she made little sleeping sounds before she managed to tack an *Amen* onto the end.

❧

The sun shining on the worn canopy of Martha's wagon warmed her and awakened her early. "Thank You, Father," Martha prayed out loud, "for the beautiful warm day. Thank You for keeping us safe through the night, too. I love You, Father. I purely love You more than my lips can say." Josie lay on her rug on the floor of the wagon beside Martha's featherbed, which also lay on the floor. When Josie's long tongue gave her an early morning kiss, she bounded from the bed.

"Come on, Josie," she said. "Time to get moving. We have lots to do this morning. Should we go finish the clothes and let them be drying while we eat breakfast?" Josie wagged her plumy tail and Martha took that for a definite yes. She used the last of the water to wash up, then dressed in clean clothes. Maybe if she didn't get more washing she'd do her own this morning, too. Her things would be simple after what she'd been through trying to clean those filthy things in her tubs.

"Come on, Josie," Martha called, taking off down the middle of the dusty street. "I'll beat you to the creek!" Although Martha had a headstart, Josie easily beat her.

Sliding down the short bank to the creek, Martha thought it looked strange. Clean and empty. Then she knew. The clothes, tubs, pail, and everything were gone! "Where can they be?" she asked Josie in shock. "They were here last night, weren't they?" She looked up and down the creek bank. This was the spot. Wasn't it? Then she noticed the hole she'd dug to dip from. And the yellow bar of soap. This was the place all right.

Somebody had stolen her things! Including someone else's clothes! What kind of trouble was she in now? She didn't have any tubs anymore! Nor her big bucket! She sank to the clean round stones. After huddling there for a half-hour, too stunned to cry, she scrambled to her feet and turned her face heavenward. "What did I do to deserve this, Lord?" she cried out loud. "I thought You promised to be with us always. Where were You? And what am I supposed to do now?" Her strength gone, she dropped to the smooth stones again, but this time she curled into a small ball. Josie sat down, leaned against Martha, and proceeded to wash her upturned ear.

After a while, Martha reached around the big dog and pulled her close. "Oh, Josie, what would I do without you?" she asked, rubbing her pet behind the ears. As she fondled the dog, her internal tumult quieted, and she began to put this last blow into perspective. Yes, it was bad. She needed those tubs and bucket. And she had no idea what would happen when the men learned their clothes were gone. But this was nothing compared to what she'd already been through. She'd suffered the most severe blow a young person could sustain—losing Mama and Papa. And Petey, the little boy she'd cared for all the way from Independence. *Why? Why, Lord? If You'll just tell me what I'm doing wrong, I'll quit.* As she lay quietly thinking, Josie suddenly jumped away and began barking, her fur bristling.

"I thought I'd find you here," Mr. Noble said, sliding down and dropping to a sitting position beside her. "What's going on? You didn't sleep down here, did you?"

Martha popped into a sitting position. "No, but you can see we should have. Sit down, Josie. He won't bother us."

Mr. Noble looked wide-eyed at Martha, then glanced around. Finally, he nodded as if understanding her pain. "What happened to your things?"

She shrugged. He didn't respond. "The coyotes got them?" she asked with a tremulous smile.

His sympathetic chuckle rewarded her bravado. "How long have you been here?" he asked.

"We got here about sunrise."

He sat quietly a moment, then stood up. "We know who did it, of course."

"We do?"

"I threatened to hurt Slick bad if he bothered you or your dog. He thinks he can get away with this, but he can't." He stood quietly a moment. "Come on, you may as well go back to your wagon." They walked back together. When they reached the wagon, Mr. Noble showed Martha a dressed duck he'd shoved onto the wagon floor. "You go ahead and do whatever you planned. I'll see you later," he added, hurrying away.

"Thanks for the duck," she mumbled so softly he might not have heard. Do whatever she'd planned? If she didn't feel so awful, she'd laugh at that. Well, at least she didn't have to touch those filthy clothes anymore. She probably should be thankful for that. Maybe those men would never figure out who lost their clothes. That was another laugh. Didn't she just have lots to laugh about today?

She cut up the duck then remembered she needed water. In ten minutes she returned with the small drinking bucket filled to the brim. She washed the pieces of meat, put them in the kettle with a little water, and sat down to do some more thinking.

"Hello, there," a cheery voice called. "I came to visit." Martha looked up to find Nellie Martin almost beside her. Suddenly, she felt lighter.

"Hi," she returned, pointing to the two wooden boxes. "Sit down, Nellie. I'm glad to see you." Then she noticed something in Nellie's hands.

Martha's new friend handed her a piece of chocolate cake on a small, chipped, blue-bordered plate, then sat down. "Mama thought you might like this. Thought you might not have a way to bake." She took in the fire with the kettle over it. "Guess she was right."

"Thank her for me, Nellie. We'll really enjoy the cake."

"We?"

Oops. "I'll enjoy it, Nellie. I'm used to saying 'we' to my dog."

Nellie looked around some more. "Want to take a walk? Oh, I guess you're fixing something to eat. I'd better go." She stood up.

Martha stood up, too, but feeling lightheaded, sat back down. "I guess we'd better eat now, but could we take a walk afterwards?"

Nellie thought she could and after promising to come back later, left.

"Well, Josie," Martha said, "let's dig in. Thanks to Mr. Noble our flour is holding out pretty well." Martha had heard you shouldn't give dogs fowl bones as they're sharp and brittle, but she had no idea how she'd keep them from Josie. The dog ate half the duck and all the bones. Then they divided the cake. Martha got impatient when Josie swallowed her half of the cake without chewing it even once. "I may as well have eaten it all," she grumbled. "You didn't even taste it."

❧

About midafternoon, Nellie came back so the girls walked north to the creek. "Mill Creek carries a lot more water in the winter," Nellie said as they tossed small stones into the tiny stream. "Let's take off our shoes and wade."

Mill Creek. So that's what it is, Martha thought.

They both took off their shoes and stockings, held their skirts up, and waded up and down the creek, slipping on the slick rocks. Josie ran in and out of the water, exploring the dried grass, weeds, and all the delicious smells on both sides of the small stream.

"It feels nice and cool," Nellie said just before her feet went out from under her. "It's cold," she screamed, laughing, making no effort to regain her feet. ·

The girls spent an hour playing in the water, Martha being careful not to fall. How would she ever wash her clothes now? She wanted to tell Nellie about her latest calamity, but for some reason kept it to herself.

After they finished, they sat in the sun, drying, for another hour. The sun felt so good and a delicious smell, almost like ripe berries, wafted around the girls.

"What are those buildings on the other side of the creek?" Martha asked as they rested.

"Oh, you mean on past the street? That's old Fort Walla Walla where the soldiers lived during the Indian wars. In '57 they moved a couple of miles west of the street. The soldiers are still there to put down any Indian uprising. They're just not as close as they used to be."

"I see. What's going to happen to the buildings?"

Nellie shook her red head. "I don't know. Maybe someone will take them in a donation land claim." Jumping to her feet she tried to brush the wrinkles from her dress. "The sun's getting low. I'd better get back to help with supper. You can't even tell I've been wet, can you?" she asked, spinning around merrily.

Martha raised her eyebrows. "I'll bet your mother can tell," she said with an impish grin. "Will you be in big trouble?"

Nellie cocked her head, then shrugged. "She never looks at me so she won't know. But she'll notice if I don't get back to help with supper."

They hurried back, Nellie to the boardinghouse, and Martha to her covered wagon. As Martha watched her new friend disappear into the boardinghouse, she marveled at how much she'd enjoyed the day in spite of her ever increasing troubles. Maybe she'd see Nellie a lot. A good friend would make life much more bearable, even if it wouldn't bring back the missing clothes and tubs.

The sun leaned far into the west and Martha's stomach told her it was time to eat. She fixed a batch of trail bread, making a little extra as they hadn't been using it all the time lately. As she and Josie ate, she wondered if Mr. Noble had found Slick. Hopefully he had, and the missing clothes and utensils as well.

Martha's walk to Mill Creek with Nellie that afternoon had honed her curiosity, so she decided to walk south now. She'd seen some buildings in that direction and felt that she might as well investigate. Walking some distance, she discovered a few shacks widely spaced. Maybe these people had taken donation claims but she feared to venture too close. She'd ask Mr. Noble about the crude buildings the next time she saw him.

She didn't have to wait as long as she'd expected because as she neared her wagon his long frame unfolded from one of the boxes by the fire pit. "Hello," he called. "I began to think you'd grown disillusioned with our little town and left."

She laughed. "And how would I go about doing that?" She watched him a moment as he sat back down, apparently with nothing in particular to say. "Did you find my things?" she asked.

His lips stiffened into a straight line as he shook his head. "Slick's not in town today. First time since I been here."

She almost felt glad. "Well! That proves he did it."

"Not for sure. But he did it all right. Those clothes

weren't worth stealing. And no one else has it in for you."

Martha leaned forward on her box. "What about the clothes, Mr. Noble? Will they throw me in jail?"

His dark eyes sparkled. "This town don't have a jail. Wouldn't put you in one if they did." Still grinning, he shook his head. "I don't know what'll happen when they find out. The local sheriff don't have any deputies or help." He chuckled. "It's rumored he don't even have a gun. I guess it's up to the fellers who lost the clothes. You got nothing they could take and no money to pay so I guess you're all right." He stood up. "I'd better be gettin' back to my room." He stretched and looked at the western sky. "About to get dark, too." He took a few steps away from the wagon and turned back. "You just get a good sleep and don't worry none," he said. "I'll probably see you tomorrow."

Martha watched him, almost silhouetted by now, until he disappeared, not through the door, but around the boardinghouse. "Wonder what he goes around there for?" she asked Josie. Receiving one thrash of the dog's tail for an answer, she continued. "Think he's getting tired of us?" she asked. "He seemed pretty quiet this evening." She hugged the big soft head to herself. "We can't blame him. We're causing him a lot of trouble."

Something caused Josie to give a little start. Martha released her. "All right, it's not us that's causing the trouble. It's just me. C'mon, let's go to bed."

❧

Martha lay in bed, swatting at mosquitoes, when she heard men's voices. Josie bristled and a growl formed deep in her throat. Martha held the dog tight, whispering "Shhhhh" in her ear as the men stood outside the wagon, talking.

"Think she's in there?" one voice asked.

"Shore. Where else could she be?"

"Let's wake her up. She's the purtiest thing in town."

The other man snorted loudly. "Ain't a lot a wimmin to choose from, Len. But we ain't wakin' nobody up. Next time we'll just git ourselves here earlier and let the lady decide for herself which of us she likes."

Martha hardly dared breathe until the footsteps died away. Even then she feared to slap at the buzzing insects. *Please, Lord,* she pleaded silently into the darkness, *protect me until Aunt Mandy and Uncle Cleve get here. I'm getting purely scared.* She lay stiffly, controlling her breathing, for over an hour. Finally, she fell asleep holding Josie close.

six

As Abram Noble poured oats into Charity's manger box, he thought about Miss Lawford. How could she stay so sweet and calm in the face of her problems? When he was alone, her delicate face laughed into his thoughts more often than he cared to admit. Never had he seen such bright color and depth in anyone's eyes, such utterly rich dark hair, and thin straight body. She looked young. Several years younger than her age. But that might be to her advantage right now. Few men would bother a young girl.

Charity's soft nicker interrupted his thoughts. "You want more?" he asked. "You realize I haven't ridden you once in the last week? You aren't burning up much oats that way." He forked a couple of scoops of hay into the manger. The mare nibbled contentedly while Abe closed the gate and went to his room.

❧

The next morning, after breakfast, he headed to the Ball and Stone Saloon. After ordering a cup of coffee, he asked about Slick.

"Ain't seen him fer a couple o' days," the bartender said. "That's the way I like it."

Abe nodded. "Yep. Me, too, but I gotta see him. Know where he hangs out?"

The man didn't, so Abe left. He crossed the street and went into Galbraith's. Not seeing Slick, he ordered another cup of coffee. "Seen Slick around?" he asked, sipping the strong hot brew.

The man wiped the shiny board-top of the bar and shook his head. "Not for a couple o' days. Hope he's left the country."

Abe chuckled. "Well, I do and I don't. I gotta see him first. After that he don't have anything I want." He finished his coffee and headed off toward Miss Lawford's wagon. He stopped, turned around, and then headed back to the meat market. If those kinfolk didn't hurry up, that girl would be destitute. He'd help where he could. He surely did believe she'd starve before she'd take charity. Let her dog starve, too? Now that seemed a different matter. She thought more of that dog than most men did their wives.

"Why don't you just keep the paper?" he asked Chapman when the man started to wrap the rabbit.

The rustic-appearing man laughed out loud. "Abe, I took you for a man who wanted to keep things kinda clean. Losin' my knack of judgin' people, I guess." He carefully laid the paper aside for later use.

Abe couldn't help telling the man his problem with Miss Lawford. "So you see if I brought it all wrapped up, she'd refuse it right off. I don't rightly know what'll happen to that girl if her kinfolk don't get here before the snow flies."

The man winked at Abe. "You'll just have to take care of her, Abe. Now ain't that an awful pass to come to?"

Less then five minutes later, Abe walked into Miss Lawford's camp. "Did you find him?" she asked right off.

He shook his head. "Not yet, but I will. He can't get along without his booze forever." He held out the rabbit. "Guess I'm too late for your breakfast."

"Yes, but I'll put it in some water and we'll have it for supper." She flashed him a radiant smile. "I can't thank you enough, Mr. Noble. Your extra meat helps us so much." She looked into his eyes. "It *is* extra, isn't it?"

He assured her he'd had all he could eat for breakfast.

She nodded. "Good. Oh, yes, Mr. Noble. I have something I've been wanting to ask you." She pointed south and east of them. "Do you know what's going on out there? I saw some buildings. Think they could be people getting donation claims?"

He nodded thoughtfully. He needed to get busy and find the perfect spot for his claim. Why had he been dillydallying, anyway? He didn't know what, but something seemed to keep him from moving ahead with his longed-for plans. Well, yes, he did too know what. He kept trying to figure a way to get Miss Lawford on the claim next to his. It looked impossible though. She lacked a lot of years of being old enough.

Miss Lawford's voice brought Abe to the present. "Is there any way I could find out about the shacks?"

"We could go ask them."

Her face colored. "Oh, I didn't mean that. I'd be afraid to bother anyone."

He got up. "I'm not. I'll go get Charity and we'll have ourselves a little ride. She's been needing some exercise, anyway. Might be interesting." He hurried away, forgetting to say goodbye.

୬

The mare nickered when Abe entered the barn as if glad to see him. "Well, you're goin' to get to see a little of the country around here," he told her as he threw the saddle over her back and cinched it up. "Think you're up to a heavy load for a while?" he asked, gently inserting the bit between her teeth. Charity nuzzled his neck as he took the reins and led her out the door. Outside, he swung into the saddle as if he were used to it. And he was. He and Charity had ridden lots of miles together when he'd been in the army. He patted the shiny neck as they turned toward the wagon.

He wouldn't mind at all sitting close to Miss Lawford for a little while. He patted Charity again. "I'll be careful not to overload you though," he whispered softly.

Then Miss Lawford and Josie ran to meet them. "He has a horse, Josie, a beautiful horse," he heard her say as they ran.

"Whoa," Abe said softly, taking the slack from the reins. When Charity stopped, he slid off. "Ready, Miss Lawford? I'll help you aboard."

Martha looked at the trim horse. "What about you, sir?" she asked.

"I'm riding, too. I wouldn't do it if you weren't so tiny, even though everyone else treats their horses that way. A horse shouldn't carry more than ten percent of its own weight. I've seen three people pile onto a horse, then force it to gallop. I've seen horses with bad swaybacks, too. I've even seen people force horses to run until they died." He stopped with a jerk. "Well, I didn't mean to get going on that," he said, puffing. "We'll just take good care of Charity here."

Miss Lawford moved back a few feet. "I can walk," she said. "Josie and I'll just walk along beside you."

"No. Charity won't mind for a little while. We won't run her and we won't go very far."

"Sure?"

"Sure. Get over here." He settled her behind the saddle, then easily swung himself up, doubling his leg as it cleared

the saddle, so it didn't bump Miss Lawford. He handled
the reins gently and Charity turned south. "You just put
your arms around me," he said. "I got stirrups to hold me
and you don't."

"We could have all walked. It isn't far at all." Miss
Lawford reached her thin arms around him but Abe could
barely feel her. She must be reluctant to be so close. And
to touch him.

He nodded. "You just hang on tight, Miss Lawford.
You could crack a bone if you fell off. I know we could
have walked and enjoyed it." He grinned and wiped his
forehead. "I don't know why but a horse gives a man a
little authority." He leaned forward and stroked the sleek
neck. "You'll be all right, won't you, girl?" He looked
east and pointed. "You mean those buildings there?"

"Yes. And a few more."

Turning the mare eastward, they walked straight to one
of the ramshackle buildings, Josie running and frolicking
alongside. "Whoa," Abe said softly, pulling his leg awk-
wardly back so he wouldn't kick Miss Lawford as he slid
off then helped her down. She took hold of Josie's collar.

A man, who'd been digging with a shovel, looked up.
"I c'n do somethin' for you folks?" he asked.

"Yes, sir," Abe answered. "We're interested in a donation claim and wondered if that's what you have here."

The man pushed the shovel into the ground with his
foot and let it stand. "Shore is." He spun around looking
at the vast expanse of dried grass and tall weeds. "Ain't it
a beaut though? Got me three hundred twenty acres. A
year from now I'll be harvesting wheat or somethin'."

"I guess I'll have to be satisfied with one hundred sixty
acres," Abe said. "But that's a lot, too."

The man glanced at Abe, then Martha, and shook his

head. "You can get the same as me and my woman if you hurry. Who knows what they'll do next year."

Abe and the man talked a few minutes discussing the steps involved in taking a donation claim, then Abe said they should be getting back.

When they reached some distance from the man's place, Abe turned the horse toward another shack south and off to the west. Charity walked sedately to the shanty and Abe climbed off. Miss Lawford slid off before he could help her, called Josie, and held her collar. A woman opened the door with a child on each side, hanging onto her skirt. "You'uns want somethin'?" she asked in a trembly voice that sounded fearful.

"We just stopped to say hello," Abe answered, hoping he sounded harmless. "I'm hoping to get a donation claim, and we're just talking to people, finding out what we can."

The woman nodded, pushing back the strands of grayish hair that had fallen loose. "That's what we got here. Rube isn't here. He could tell you about it better'n I can."

"That's all right. How can you tell where your property ends?"

The woman finally smiled. "It goes on a long ways. Three hundred twenty acres we got ourselves here."

Abe cast a glance at Miss Lawford. "Thanks for taking the time to talk to us. Maybe we'll be neighbors one of these days."

After another short ride they stopped at a raggedy tent and dismounted.

"Looks pretty quiet," Miss Lawford murmured. "I wonder if anyone's around." She took Josie's collar. For the first time the dog pulled against her and growled. Martha's hand tightened on the collar.

Just then a matted gray head poked through the canvas

doorway. "Whatcha want?" he asked.

Abe almost choked when he recognized Slick's thin voice. "We came to see you, Slick. Better come out."

After a long wait the filthy man pushed the canvas door aside and stepped out. Miss Lawford stepped back ten feet; Abe almost did, too. How the man could stand to be in a small unventilated tent with himself, Abe couldn't imagine.

"Where are the things you took from the creek?" Abe asked.

Slick blinked. "What things you talkin' about?" he asked.

"You know what I'm talking about, Slick." Abe's voice didn't sound so harmless anymore. "You bring them out or I'm coming in after them."

Slick backed up a few feet. "I don't know what you're talking about, boy, but you got the wrong man. I been right here tryin' to git over the flu for almost a week."

Abe shoved the canvas tent door apart with both hands and stepped inside. It took a moment for his eyes to adjust, and the smell turned his stomach. Dirty clothes covered a filthy looking sleeping bag. Several tin dishes lay scattered over the dirt floor. Then he saw the tubs and bucket. Stacked neatly inside each other, they appeared to be the cleanest articles in the smelly tent. Abe grabbed them up and carried them outside. Setting them down, he backed off and took several deep breaths. "How do you stand yourself and that tent?" he asked. "That smell's enough to knock a good man down."

Slick pointed at the tubs and bucket. "What you doin' with them things?"

"We're taking them. They belong to Miss Lawford. Where's the clothes, Slick? She'll be in trouble if she doesn't return the clothes."

Slick snatched at the utensils. "Them's mine and you ain't takin 'em nowhere," he whined.

Abe met Miss Lawford's eyes. "Are they yours?"

She stepped over and looked at each one separately. "Each of my three are different and these're just like mine. Strange he'd have three exactly like mine." She shrugged. "But I don't know."

Abe nodded. "Yep. A little too much coincidence. Look here, Slick, are you ready to stop messing with Miss Lawford? I'm about to send you out of town faster than you came in. No one in this town would cry, neither." He picked up the bucket and stack of tubs and set them down beside Charity. "Come on, Miss Lawford, let's get you up there." A moment later he picked up the things again, swung into the saddle and held the large pieces of equipment to his side. "Come on, Charity, just a little farther."

As the horse moved away, Josie, growling deep in her throat, jumped on two feet toward Slick. Slick screamed. Before Abe could move, Miss Lawford hit the ground and threw herself onto the big dog.

"Josie, stop," she said, grasping the dog's collar. Josie yielded to Martha's touch, calming down. "You go on, Mr. Noble," she called. "I'll have to bring Josie."

Abe wheeled Charity around between Slick and the girl. "All right," he said softly. "You go on. I'll be right behind you." He turned to Slick, whose eyes still bulged half out of his head. "I'm not warning you again," he told the man. "This is it. Next time you cause either of us any trouble you're out of here. Come on, Charity, let's go find some air we can breathe." He turned the already prancing horse and took off at a gallop after Martha.

seven

Early the next morning, Mr. Noble brought Martha another rabbit. "Josie and I can't thank you enough," she said. "Where you getting them, anyway? I watched last night and didn't see a thing."

Mr. Noble smiled. "You think they'd come out with Josie there?"

She nodded as she cut up the meat and put it into the kettle to boil.

"Say," he said, "I found the perfect place for a claim. How'd you like to see it one of these days? It's just a little ways. You can ride Charity and I'll walk with Josie."

"Mr. Noble, why don't we both walk? I'd enjoy it. If you have that much time, that is."

"We'll see. Charity would enjoy having you ride her, though. Do you like to ride?"

Martha nodded enthusiastically. "I love to ride. But not when I make the horse's owner walk."

Mr. Noble hurried back to town. Martha took the rabbit from the water, cooled it, and divided it with Josie. After they finished she let Josie drink the cooled juice the rabbit had been cooked in. The dog licked the kettle so clean that Martha couldn't find a drop on it.

She'd just finished washing the dishes and kettle when two men rode up. The brown-and-white spotted horses they rode hardly compared with Mr. Noble's sleek bay mare.

"You the girl who's washing our clothes?" the dark

55

whiskery one asked. Neither man dismounted.

Suddenly, Martha felt so lightheaded she had to sit on one of the boxes. Why hadn't she prepared for this meeting? It had to happen. *Help me, Lord. Show me what to say and don't let them get mad at me.* The men didn't really look mean, but everyone around looked tough. Then she noticed their filthy clothes. They owned the clothes all right. Their overalls looked just as filthy as the ones she'd lost. But what could she say? Well, Mama had always taught her the truth was the easiest and best.

She cleared her throat and hung tightly to Josie's collar. "Yes sir, I am."

The dark-haired man nodded. "Any idea when they'll be ready? Folks around here don't have too many clothes."

Her mother's voice spoke plainly into her ear. *Tell the man the truth, Martha!* She nodded. *Yes, Mama. You're right.* "I'm afraid I have real bad news about your clothes, sir."

The younger fellow with the light-colored, shaggy hair gave a short laugh. "What? Them clothes was so dirty they fell apart when you washed them! I figgered that'd happen."

Martha couldn't help giving him a little smile. Then she shook her head. "They didn't fall apart. They totally disappeared." Seeing their surprise, she went on. "I had to wash them at the creek because they were so dirty and took so much water. I washed them twice the day I got them then left them soaking overnight on the creek bank and when I went back the next morning they were gone . . .and I don't know what to do." She took a long deep breath.

The horses moved a little in the silence that followed Martha's outburst. She could see sympathy in the younger man's eyes. Maybe the older one, too.

"I'm sorry to hear that," the older man said. "You got any plans to find the clothes? And what ya gonna do if you can't find 'em?"

Martha found some strength and stood beside the man's horse. "I don't know yet, sir. I don't have any money. That's why I was washing clothes."

The man turned his horse. "We'll be back in a few days to see what you figgered out. When someone goes into business, 'e usually knows what 'e's doin'." He touched his horse's sides and they tore off toward the street.

Martha released Josie's collar. "Well, what's going to happen to us?" she asked the shaggy dog. "I guess they still don't have a jail." She went inside the wagon and looked at the calendar she'd made. She checked off today. *Thanks for being with me, God. I was purely scared. Are you watching over Aunt Mandy and Uncle Cleve, Lord? They should be here by now, and I'm getting into a worse mess all the time. Please bring them soon. I need them, and Jackson, too.* She didn't know if Jackson, her older brother, had met the wagon train her uncle, aunt, and cousin were with. He should have by now. He really should have, and they should be coming down off the Blue Mountains already.

❧

That night, rain splattering on the wagon canopy woke Martha. She snuggled deeper into her covers. Hopefully the top would keep her dry. It had before during a light rain. Then she remembered the times every wagon had to be emptied so everything could be set out to dry. What a mess! She dropped her arm over Josie who slept beside her, and fell back to sleep.

But she awakened again sometime later, cold and wet.

She couldn't do anything in the dark and had no place to go where she'd be out of the rain. She pulled Josie into her bed and put Josie's rug over them. The dog helped warm her some, and the rug helped a little, but before long both dog and girl were thoroughly chilled. As she lay holding the dog close she wondered what she'd do in the morning.

She must have fallen asleep, for she awakened with a start to face daylight. A moment later she noticed she didn't hear rain anymore. "What are we going to do, Josie?" she asked her wet but warm pet. "At least you don't have to put on cold wet clothes. Well, you don't, because you're wearing them."

"Are you in there, Miss Lawford?" Mr. Noble's soft voice called through the soaked cloth wagon top.

Oh, oh. Now she not only had to get into wet clothes but she had to do it in a hurry. "I'm here," she called. "I'll be out in a minute." Josie didn't have anything holding her back so she jumped down, eager to greet her new friend.

Martha could hardly bear to take off her warm wet nightgown and put on her cold wet clothes. Everything stuck to her but she finally got changed. Then she brushed her hair, braided it, and put it up.

Martha jumped to the ground to find it had turned to mud during the downpour. After a quick feeling of defeat she looked up to find Mr. Noble watching her.

"I knew you'd get soaked," he said. "You can't stay out here much longer you know. It's going to rain a few times, then it'll turn to snow." He had a rabbit in his hand but didn't offer it to her. "You're freezing right now, aren't you? Come to the boardinghouse with me before you catch pneumonia."

She couldn't do that! She couldn't get more indebted to this man than she already was. She'd been writing down all the meat he brought and what she thought it would be worth if she'd bought it. But she'd never be able to pay a boardinghouse bill. Never!

"I'll be just fine," she said, trying to smile through chattering teeth. "As soon as I get a fire going I'll get warm." She pointed toward the east. "The sun's going to shine, too. Just you wait and see."

"Let me help you get the fire started then." He jumped into the wagon, returning a moment later with a handful of buffalo chips. After working for some time, the chips caught fire. Wordlessly, he picked the rabbit off the box he'd laid it on and handed it to her.

She washed the rabbit and cut it up, then dumped it into the kettle to cook.

"Do you get tired of eating the same thing all the time?"

She flashed a nice smile. "When I'm not so impoverished I'll worry about getting tired of something. Right now I'm happy to have anything for Josie and me to eat." She sat down on the box, hoping the fire would dry her clothes.

He sat down on the other box. "I hate to bring this up, Miss Lawford, but it seems to me your kin should be here by now. Anytime now the Blue Mountains will be blocked with snow, lots of snow. It might have snowed up there last night."

Martha's heart shrank a little in her chest. She knew even better than he did what a terrible position she was in. She couldn't hold back a strong burst of shivering. "I don't know where they are but they have to come soon. They just have to." She blinked hard. She wouldn't cry. Not in front of Mr. Noble.

He got to his feet. "I'm leaving for a while. I'll be back." He stood quietly, just looking at her for a moment. "You have to face the facts, Miss Lawford. If you insist on staying here in the wagon, I'll come out here some morning and find you with pneumonia or worse. As if you aren't in enough trouble, you're out of chips." He turned and strode toward his boardinghouse.

eight

Abe slammed up to his room, hardly seeing Nellie, and not speaking as he passed her. He tipped up one side of the chiffonier and grabbed his money pouch from under it. Dropping to the bed, he dumped the contents on the smooth quilt. Barely noticing the gold pieces, Miss Lawford's delicate but cold form thrust itself into his mind. He'd never seen anyone so brave—man, woman, or child. Those brilliant blue eyes had sparkled with unshed tears this morning but she'd held them back.

His eyes clouded as he wondered if she were crying now with no one but Josie to see and comfort her. He simply couldn't handle the way things were going for Martha Lawford. Something had to be done. Now!

He sat up and stacked his $100 gold pieces in piles of ten. He hadn't used any of them since he got here so he still had thirty. Then his $50 nuggets. Nine of those. His paper money and coins added up to $337. He pulled out a piece of paper and pencil and added his figures—$3787. And then there was the $490 he kept in the top drawer as a decoy. He gave all the pieces an angry shove, jumbling them together. He had plenty of money to last until he could begin making more. Why couldn't he use some of it to help Miss Lawford? Ever since he'd met the girl he'd thought of almost nothing else. She was everything he'd ever wanted in a woman, so why was she sitting outside in the cold and rain while he had a warm dry room?

"Show me how, Lord," he cried. "I don't want her to

suffer or get sick and die! You don't, either, Lord. I know You don't! Please show me how to help her."

Sadly shoving his money back into the pouch, he once again lifted the chiffonier and laid the bag under so it didn't show. He sat on the edge of the bed, his chin cupped in his hands and his elbows on his knees, deep in thought.

You could marry her, Abe. He could marry her! He could marry her and take care of her! In his elation, he jumped to his feet.

Then he sank back to the bed. What made him think she'd ever have him? She was scared to death of men—the sex to which he had to claim membership. More than once she'd shrunk away from him when he'd accidentally touched her. And she'd never given him the slightest reason to think she felt anything for him, other than gratitude.

"That's not it, Lord. She'd never do it. Even if she wasn't fearful, she's plenty proud. She'd call it charity." He shook his head thinking about it. There had to be another way.

You really could marry her. He shook his head again.

Then a new thought popped up. The I and R building wasn't occupied. Maybe he could rent that for her and fix it up. "Yeah!" he said out loud, finally wearing a wide smile. "Thanks, Lord," he said, not realizing the Lord hadn't said anything about renting a building for her.

But the owner of the building planned to open his own business in it almost immediately.

Abe left, dejected. As he crossed back to his place he decided he might as well check on Miss Lawford to see if he could do anything to help her dry out her wagon and things.

When he turned west, he thought his eyes were playing

tricks on him—three wagons stood where only one had this morning. Probably her kinfolks! He tore off to the wagons at top speed, trying to decide if he really was all that happy they'd come. Would she decide she didn't need him anymore?

Arriving, he found several children playing around the wagons, ten oxen grazing on the nearly dried grass and weeds, and four adults talking to Miss Lawford. Several substantial pieces of wood lay on the ground beside the blazing fire. Every sturdy weed in the area supported some article of clothing or bedding.

"Hello, Mr. Noble," Miss Lawford called. "Come meet my new friends."

He soon learned Miss Lawford hadn't known them until an hour or two ago. "Where you headin'?" he asked after a while.

The men laughed cheerfully. "We ain't heading nowheres," the short one said. "We just found it. Ain't this what they call the land of many waters?"

Abe nodded. "Reckon as how some do. Got several streams running around the place. It's also called Steptoeville or Waiilapptu."

"We're collecting us some donation land claims," Wilford, the tall one said. "Miss Martha tells us we can get three hundred twenty acres each. That's enough for us."

"Did you folks get wet last night?" Abe asked.

The women shook their heads. "We spent the night near the burned out mission. Nary a drop did it rain." She smiled at Miss Lawford and patted her arm. "Sure got Martha, though."

Unkind thoughts skittered around in Abe's mind. These people just arrived this morning. How did they have the right to call Miss Lawford by her Christian name already? Did she invite them to? She sure hadn't told him he could. He forced his mind back to the company. "I see you got your things drying, Miss Lawford," he said. "Sure hope it don't rain again until your kin gets here." He turned to the standing men again. "I guess you folks don't know anything about her kinfolk's wagon train."

They both shook their heads. "No," Wilford said. "We just come from the Willamette Valley. I reckon we'll be finding us some claims and moving onto 'em purty soon. Gonna have to work fast to get cabins built before bad weather comes."

Abe nodded. "Sure are. I'm doing the same thing. Gotta quit messing around and get busy myself." He started away from the wagon. "See you again, Miss Lawford. Glad you're getting dried out."

"Thanks again, Mr. Noble," Miss Lawford said. She giggled softly. "I'd likely be dead if you hadn't helped me so much."

ᴥ

Those people would no doubt be telling Miss Lawford right now to watch out for him, he thought, rushing back to his room. He sat in the rickety rocking chair in the corner of the room, thinking.

He really should go ahead and get his claim settled and build his own cabin.

Marry her, Abe. Abe thoroughly liked the idea. That would solve all their joint problems. She'd be able to get a claim now while they were still available. She wouldn't be out in the cold and rain with nothing to eat. He'd be able to care for her as he longed to do. It hurt him deep inside to see her suffering so. Then with a shock he realized he loved her! He'd loved her almost since they first met.

He looked up and discovered he'd been rocking furiously. Slowing to a sensible pace, he smiled. He loved Martha! What a beautiful name for a beautiful girl, inside and out. A girl with plenty of pluck. He shook his head. He couldn't file his claim without her. He'd talk to her the first time he got her alone.

Then he remembered he'd promised to take her to the spot he'd found for the claim. Maybe he could get her away from the others to go look. He grabbed his hat, tore down the stairs, and ran out the door.

"I just remembered inviting you to go see a purty parcel of land," he said when she came to meet him. They'd stopped a few feet from the others. "Think you could get away for a little while to see it?"

She glanced toward the others and shook her head. "I don't know. What do you think?"

He smiled into her sincere blue eyes. "I dunno," he said. "Are you entertaining them? Or are they just waiting to file their claims?"

She grabbed his arm. "Can we go right now?" He nodded. "I'll be back in a little while," she called to the people around her wagon. "Come on, Josie."

He led her south of the buildings, then east behind them. "It's right on Mill Creek," he said, cutting back southeast.

In a few minutes they stood on the bank of the small stream. Trees lined the creek bank almost until it reached the street. Probably people had cut those in the way of the street. He turned south and held his arms out to his sides, his hands facing the property. His heart thrilled every time he stood in that spot. "Well, what do you think?" he asked.

She looked. She looked up and down the creek, then

her eyes moved over the large expanse of land. "It's the most beautiful piece of land I've ever laid eyes on," she said quietly. "I purely wish I could get a piece right beside you. Oh, how I wish I were twenty-one!"

Abe wanted more than anything in the world to ask her to marry him. And she'd made it so easy. He could tell her she could have her 160 acres right now. He could tell her he'd take care of her forever. He could tell her he loved her! Her deep blue eyes gazed into his, her full lips slightly parted, waiting. But he couldn't get the words past the mountain-sized lump in his throat. He tried several times but nothing came out.

"Come on," he finally croaked. "Let's get you back to your friends."

Leaving her just before they reached the other people, Abe decided he might as well look around some more; at least he'd be giving Charity some exercise.

nine

Martha stood where Mr. Noble had left her and watched him stride down the street. He'd been in a strange mood. First he'd been jolly and talkative, then he hushed right up. She hoped she hadn't offended him in some way. Well, she'd better get back to her new friends.

"Say, is that fellow more than a friend?" Mr. Tynnon asked. He shoved his stringy blond hair back and grinned at Martha.

She shook her head. "Just a friend, but the best friend anyone could have. Why do you ask?"

Mrs. Tynnon stepped over to Martha. "Honey, didn't you see how he looked at you? That man had stars in his eyes."

Martha shrugged. "You misread him, Mrs. Tynnon. He's just a really good man."

"Why did he have to take you off alone then?" Mrs. Nelson asked. "He's sweet on you, young lady, and a mighty fine looking man he is, too. You won't find any better in a small place like this. Maybe not anywhere."

"Mind if we stay the night here with you?" Mr. Tynnon asked. "Tomorrow we can find our claims and get out of your way."

"That would be nice," Mrs. Tynnon added. "We could get—Timothy, drop those clothes!"

Martha looked to see the little boy dragging across the muddy grass most of her clothes as well as her bedding with Josie on the other end. She jumped up and rescued them. Only a little muddy, she put them away before they got worse. Shoving them into the wagon, she decided she could fold them later.

"I'm sorry I can't invite you for supper," she told the visitors. "I have only a wee bit of flour to eat. I mix it with water and call it trail bread but I have only about a quart left."

Mrs. Nelson made a face. "That's all right," she said too quickly. "We'll just share the fire. You go ahead first, child, and when you're through we'll cook our meal."

Embarrassed, Martha mixed some water into half her flour and cooked it in her pot.

"That stuff smells funny," one of the children said as it cooked; his mother told him to hush.

When the bread was ready, Martha divided it with Josie, who gulped it down without complaint. Just as Martha had finished eating, the two men whose clothes she'd lost, rode up.

"Howdy," the older one said, tipping his ragged, filthy hat. "Your kinfolks finally got here, I see."

Martha shook her head. "No, these folks came from Oregon City. My aunt and uncle will be here in a few days."

Mrs. Tynnon smiled again. "In the morning we're going to find ourselves some donation land claims."

"Congratulations, I'm sure." He reined his horse around until he faced Martha again. "What have you figured out, Miss Lawford?"

Martha shook her head. "I didn't find the clothes. . .and I still don't have any money." Suddenly, she remembered her father's clothes in the wagon. Although she felt sentimental about them, she certainly didn't need them. She looked up at the big dark-haired man and smiled. "I have some clothes in the wagon you might be able to use."

Not a flicker of emotion crossed his face as he said, "Get them."

Martha clambered into the wagon, shoved aside the bunch of clothes and bedding she'd just put in, and opened the tattered black trunk. Her throat clogged as she pulled out two pairs of dress pants, three dress shirts, underwear, and five pairs of black dress socks. Hugging the garments to her chest, she realized once again that Papa would never again be with her in this world. *I needed him so much, Lord, she cried silently. When am I going to see some signs of the love I know You have for me?* She swallowed, secured a tighter grip on the clothes, and jumped to the ground.

The young blond man hadn't said a word, just sat quietly on his nervously moving horse. But when she handed the clothes to the older man the younger one burst into loud laughter. "I can just see you in that stuff," he howled through his glee.

The big man said nothing until he'd sorted through each and every garment. When he finished, he shoved the clothes back toward Martha. "Ain't a thing there a man'd wear," he growled. "Looks like preacher clothes."

Martha shook her head. "They're not," she whispered. "Those were my father's clothes. He was a farmer and these were his Sunday clothes. Don't you wear Sunday clothes sometimes?"

"Not like that stuff!" the younger man said, still laughing.

The older man glared at her for a moment, then his face softened. "I see you got the tubs back." She nodded. "The clothes weren't in them no more?"

Martha swallowed hard. "We found the tubs in a man's

tent but the clothes weren't there. We'd have taken them if we'd found them."

"Know the man's name?"

She nodded again, then wondered if she should tell. Why not? She couldn't think of any reason to protect Slick. No reason at all. "He's called Slick. That's all I know. I think Mr. Noble knows his name, though. He lives at Martin's Boardinghouse." She pointed south. "Slick's living in a tent out that way."

The man wheeled his horse away from the group. "Thanks," he grunted as the horse burst into a gallop. The younger man touched his horse's sides and took off after his friend, or father, or whatever he was. Martha shuddered as they headed south.

Martha carried the clothes back into the wagon and repacked them in the trunk. She could tell that her friends wanted to know what the men wanted but she said nothing.

Noticing the women preparing food, she climbed back into her wagon and put away her clothes and bedding. She fervently hoped she'd not endure another rainy night like she had last night while she still lived in the wagon. She jumped to the ground and saw a kettle on the fire, boiling briskly and starting to fill the area with a tantalizing fragrance. She asked what they were cooking.

"It's just a soup," Mrs. Tynnon said. "We put in some wild onions we gathered near The Dalles, some potatoes we brought from Oregon City, and dried meat and salt. Nothing special."

A little while later they called the four children and began serving up the soup, the most delicious food Martha had ever smelled in her entire life. When she decided they weren't going to offer her any, and Josie began running from one to another, begging, she called the dog and took off down the street. Just smelling the food wasn't very satisfying for either of them. She put her arm around her faithful friend's neck as they walked. "I'm sorry, Josie, but those people didn't want us to have any. You just wait. One of these days you'll have all you want."

She turned right, walked past the empty building on the end of the street, and followed the creek as it turned east to the spot where she and Mr. Noble had stood earlier today. Yes! This was exactly where she'd want her farm. Exactly here. She'd put her house right over there on that little mound where it would be high and the grass would never grow brown. She looked in every direction, trying to imagine how far 160 acres would go. A long, long way.

Facing the creek, the only thing she didn't like was the sight to her left of the old abandoned Fort Walla Walla buildings. What would happen to those buildings, anyway?

She sighed and turned back to face the land Abe had shown her. How could the Garden of Eden have been more beautiful? She'd love to have this piece of ground. But it would surely be taken before she turned twenty-one. Then she laughed out loud. This place already belonged to Mr. Noble. He'd shown it to her in the first place. She cast her eyes eastward. The next place would be just as good. She'd be perfectly satisfied with it. She'd enjoy being Mr. Noble's neighbor, too. But all the good places would be taken within four years.

"You like it?"

Martha jerked around to find Mr. Noble standing behind her, looking over her shoulder at the land spreading before them. She nodded. "I even figured where to put my house before I remembered this is your piece of Washington Territory."

He swallowed and looked at her as if he were in pain . . .just as he had this afternoon. He didn't reply.

"Are you all right, sir?"

He still didn't answer but stood looking across the expanse of grass, weeds, and the few trees along the stream, his Adam's apple jiggling spasmodically. Finally, he met her eyes and smiled. "Show me where you'd build your cabin."

She laughed, a happy tinkling sound. "I said I'd build a house, sir, not a cabin." She laughed again, joyously, and ran to the small rolling knoll she'd thought to build on. "Right here," she called, standing in the middle. "Don't you think this is a good place?"

He nodded but said nothing.

"You don't like it, do you?" she asked, realizing she felt unreasonably disappointed. What difference did it make to her where he built his house. . .cabin?

After hesitating, he nodded again. "I do like it, Miss Lawford, but I thought I'd build a couple hundred feet farther up the creek." He beckoned with his hand and she followed him, feeling nice and warm in the autumn sun and realizing the luxury of the feeling.

He finally stopped on another small rise. "How's this?" he asked, his soft brown eyes boring into hers.

She nodded. "Fine, except there aren't any trees."

"I'll plant some," he said, his eyes starting to get their usual sparkle again. "Fruit trees, shade trees, and whatever else you. . .I mean *I* want."

Martha couldn't be sure but she thought Mr. Noble's tanned face turned rosy. "I don't know much about trees," she said, "but I like these that our Lord planted. They look just right."

He nodded. "I think they're locust trees. I could probably find some small ones and bring them over here and replant them. I'd have to do it a little later when they're sleeping."

"That sounds good. Well, Josie and I'd better be getting back to the wagon." She met his soft brown eyes again. "I'm not sure why but I like it alone better than with those folks."

"They leaving soon?"

"Tomorrow they say."

"All right. I'll probably see you then." He hesitated a moment then turned to follow her. "I might as well see you get back to the wagon safe."

Neither talked as they walked behind the buildings, Josie running circles around them. Martha's thoughts kept going back to one pint of flour and no buffalo chips at all. And those people knew it and didn't offer her anything at all. But they had a lot of people to feed and maybe they didn't have much food either. Maybe.

Mr. Noble stopped before they reached the wagons. "I'll go back now," he said. "I hope you'll enjoy your guests tonight."

"Thanks," she said. "Goodbye." She turned, dreading to have to spend the evening with the Nelsons and Tynnons. Maybe she'd go to bed early. Last night had been bad and she hadn't gotten much sleep.

"Well," Mrs. Nelson said with apparent glee, "look who brought you home."

"What did he do, take you out for an ice cream?" Mr. Tynnon asked.

Martha laughed. "I'm afraid you won't find any ice cream in Steptoeville. This is just a little western settlement. Maybe some day you'll find fancy things, but not yet." She stretched. "I hope you won't mind if I go to bed early. I didn't get much sleep last night and I'm tired. Come on, Josie."

≈

The next morning Martha built a fire with the newcomers' wood and made the last of her flour into trail bread, trying to forget the lovely smells from last night. As always, she shared her meager meal with Josie, who swallowed the small bit and begged for Martha's half. Martha chucked it down as quickly as she could. "I'd give it to you, Josie," she whispered, "but I'm already weak from not eating."

The occupants from the other wagons still slept so Martha and Josie walked to the creek again, following it south then east for some distance. The bright sun on her shoulders made her feel good even though she literally didn't know from where her next meal would come.

They walked farther east than she and Mr. Noble had last night and she found trees bordering the creek again. Trying to see everything, she decided this land was even prettier than Mr. Noble's.

After she felt completely alone, she knelt by the bubbling stream.

"Thank You for the warm sunshine, Lord," she said out loud. Josie came and sat beside her, licking her closest cheek. "Two days ago I didn't appreciate it but now I realize what a precious blessing it is. Six months ago I didn't even appreciate good food, but I do now. Oh, I really do now. Lord, You know how it is with me and I know You have something planned so Josie and I won't starve, but we're both hungry now. We'll try our best to be patient if that's what You want, and if we're doing something to displease You, show us, Lord, so we can stop. I love You, God, and purely want to please You. Thank You for Your past care, and Your future care, too. We pray in Jesus' name. Amen."

She sat on the bank of the creek, her arms wrapped around her knees, enjoying the busy sound of the stream rushing over the rocks, the bird calls from the meadow floor, and the warm sun on her back.

Somehow her mind went back to the long, long trip over the Oregon Trail. She thought of the times when they traveled several days without water, without either water or feed for the stock. And the times the oxen dropped in their harnesses and died on the spot. And the crossings of the Snake River. They'd thought that some of the other streams were hard, but they didn't know hard until they crossed the mighty Snake.

They'd lost a yoke of oxen when it had been swept down the wild stream, and one wagon had been turned over and destroyed. But worst of all was that a little five-year-old boy had drowned. A little boy she'd played with and helped care for during the entire trip.

Just before that, Mama had sickened, and then Papa had come down with it the day before Mama had died. He'd never known she died. In fact, he'd thought Martha had been Mama the last day of his life.

Martha bowed her head into the circle of her arms as they lay on her knees. *It's been hard, Lord. And it's still bad. What should I do? Even out here in nowhere land there has to be a way to get food for Josie and me. I'm willing to work hard. Just show me, Lord, and I'll do it. Anything.*

She sat quietly until Josie nuzzled her arm and made a sound half between a bark and a growl. Martha lifted her head and laughed. "You're telling me to get up and get going, aren't you, Josie? Well, let's go." She scrambled to her feet, giving the big dog several pats in passing, then pulled up her skirts and took off running back toward town. She'd stop at every business and ask for work.

She found rough men in every building. The two whose clothes she'd lost seemed to own the tin shop. They, as well as all the rest acted like gentlemen, and expressed sorrow over having to decline her application for work. Most of them ran their own businesses and barely made a living without hiring anyone.

The barkeeps told her they'd be afraid to hire her for her own safety, that there weren't half a dozen women in town. When she left the last building, feeling depressed, she noticed her wagon stood alone.

"Josie," she said, taking off running, "they're gone." She stopped running and stood looking at her wagon. "I didn't think I'd ever be happy to be alone, but I am." She hurried to the wagon. Then she remembered she had nothing to eat and no way to make a fire even if Mr. Noble brought her something. "At least we'll be alone so we can starve in peace, won't we, Josie?" she asked, still feeling lighthearted for some strange reason. She had no food, she'd just learned there was no work for her in Steptoeville, and she felt happy? She remembered reading in the Bible how the birds didn't work, nor the lilies of the field, but God took care of them. Then it went on to say how much more valuable people are than birds or flowers. That meant her. God loved her more than the birds or lilies.

She sat down on one of the dynamite boxes to rest, feeling she'd had a busy morning although she'd done nothing but learn there was no work for her. . .and remember the awful trip west. She fell deep into her thoughts again and didn't hear the horses until they almost reached her.

"Whoa, Charity," Mr. Noble's soft voice murmured. "You got no call to be skittish with Sampson." He stepped down from the saddle and led the two horses up to the wagon.

Martha met him. "You have another horse, Mr. Noble. It's beautiful just like Charity."

Mr. Noble smiled. "Nah, he ain't like Charity. She's a lady through and through. He's just an old nag I picked up."

ten

In his excitement, Abe's legs barely held him up. In the few days he'd been looking, he'd been lucky to find another horse of Charity's quality. Darker than Charity and with a creamy mane, tail, and socks, the horse made a pretty sight. Martha had to like him. He stood two hands taller than Charity and, though spirited, he'd be easy for her to ride.

"Come ride with me," he said, holding his breath for fear she'd refuse. He'd made up his mind that today he'd ask her to marry him. No matter what, he'd do it this time.

She shook her head. "I don't know if I should," she said. "Besides, you don't have a sidesaddle."

"A sidesaddle? Come on, Miss Lawford. No one out here uses a sidesaddle. Don't you know they're dangerous? That dress you have on is plenty full to be perfectly modest."

Miss Lawford's clear blue eyes looked questioning as though it might not be proper.

"I have something important to do," he said, hoping to tempt her. "Somebody beat Slick Collier almost to death. I found him in front of the saloon this morning and hauled him out to Fort Walla Walla. I need to see if he's still alive."

Miss Lawford's eyes opened wide, her face paled, then her hand flew to her mouth.

"Why do you act like that?" he asked.

She opened her mouth to speak then shook her head. "I better come with you," she said. "Will you teach me to ride straddle?"

Abe laughed. "You'll know how right off, and wonder how you ever stayed on that sidesaddle. After one ride you'll never sit one of them crazy things again."

"Let's get me on then. Is the horse friendly?"

"Yeah, he's great." He met her eyes for just a second. "Don't think I'd let you ride him if he wasn't, do you? Here, put your left foot in the stirrup and I'll boost you as you swing up." She did as he instructed and sat in the saddle as if she'd been riding straddle forever.

Sampson danced a little but quieted when she gently firmed the reins and talked to him. "I feel as if I'm on top of the world," she said to Abe. "He's awfully big."

Feeling secure in the way she handled the big chestnut, Abe mounted Charity. "How you doing? Want to take it easy for a while?" he called over his shoulder to Miss Lawford.

"Oh, Mr. Noble, I love him. I purely love him. We're doing fine and we're ready to do whatever you do."

Abe touched Charity's sides with his knees. "Come on, girl, let's hurry," he said softly. The sleek horse stretched her front feet forward into a long lope that covered the ground in a hurry. Behind him, Miss Lawford called Josie to come along. The less than two miles would have been a nice run for the horses, but after a half-mile Abe reigned Charity in and Miss Lawford and Sampson slowed   beside him.

"I love Sampson," she said, "and I love the speed, but I'm glad we slowed because Josie's not strong enough right now to run very far."

In a few minutes the dog caught up and trotted beside

Miss Lawford and Sampson, her tongue hanging out the side of her mouth. No need to mention that Josie was the reason Abe had slowed to a walk.

"How far out is Fort Walla Walla?" Miss Lawford asked.

"We're almost there," Abe replied.

"Do you have any idea what happened to Slick?" she asked.

He shook his head. "Someone beat him to a bloody mess. Beyond that, not a hunch. Do you know something?" She didn't answer but he had a gut feeling she did. Why didn't she tell him?

As they rode quietly along, he stole quick peeks at her. Just the curve of her chin and neck left him breathless, as did the long dark lashes over her bright eyes. "You ride like you been riding straddle forever," he said. "How d'you like it?"

"You're right. It's the way to ride." She looked behind them. "Come on, Josie, just a little farther."

Abe saw the Fort Walla Walla buildings and pointed. "There's the fort. We're here already."

In a few minutes someone invited them into one of the log buildings and called a doctor to talk to them. They waited on a rough bench in a big room with tables, probably the eating hall. Several braided rugs covered most of the unfinished wooden floor.

Finally, a very tall man dressed in buckskins and having long brown hair that curled on the ends, a full beard, and a thick mustache approached. "You related to Slick Collier?"

"No, I'm the one who found him and brought him out here. Didn't know what else to do with him. How is he?"

The doctor shook his head. "I didn't find any broken

bones, but he's barely breathing. I guess we'll just have to let him rest and see what happens." He stopped and drew a couple of breaths. "Learn anything about what happened?"

Abe shook his head then glanced at Martha. . .Miss Lawford. Why did he keep using her Christian name in his mind? Pretty soon he'd do it to her face and that might mess things up. And why didn't she tell the man what she knew?

She said nothing.

"How long before you have an idea whether he'll make it?" Abe asked.

The doctor shrugged. "Dunno. Maybe tomorrow, maybe a week."

Abe got to his feet and shook hands with the doctor again. "We'll probably be back tomorrow."

*

As Martha and Abe took their time returning to the wagon, Josie, who had recovered some, trotted beside the horses. "Think Josie'd stay at the wagon if we went for a longer ride?" Abe asked when they neared Steptoeville.

She shook her head. "Not unless we tied her or something. She thinks she's my guard."

When they reached Miss Lawford's wagon, Abe looped the horses' reins over the tongue of the wagon. "I got a couple of things to ask you about," he said. "You got time to talk?"

She laughed. "No, I'm sorry, sir, but I have a formal ball to attend tonight. Would you like to make an appointment for next week?"

He grinned back at her, turned the boxes upright, and shoved one toward her. "Sassy little thing, ain't you? Well, I need to hear what you know about Slick's accident."

She sighed, hesitated a moment, then answered. "I thought you'd ask me before the day ended." She wound her hands around each other then released them. "I don't know for sure, but I have an idea." She told him about the men whose clothes Slick had stolen, and about her telling them who'd taken them and where he lived. "It looks like they beat him, don't you think?"

"No!" Abe said, louder than he meant to. "Those boys are tough but they'd never hurt anyone." But even as he denied it, he came to feel she was right. "Well, what do we do about it?" he asked.

"I don't know what happened," Miss Lawford said. "Why don't you talk to the men?"

Abe thought a moment, then shook his head. After all, he'd given Slick a licking, too. Slick seemed to provoke a man to do that. First and foremost in his mind was what he wanted to ask Miss Lawford. He grinned. "Maybe I'll just let it alone. Slick kind of affects people that way. If a chap has only two sets of clothes it might not set all that well to have someone steal one of them."

She nodded, looking as though she were a million miles away. He got up. "Reckon we could go for a walk?" he asked.

"Sure. Where?"

"I don't care."

She hopped from her box and took off south; after passing the buildings, she veered east.

Abe followed and Josie trailed after him. A few minutes later, they reached Mill Creek. She followed it south until it turned east and then followed it some more.

Finally, she stopped. "This is where I want my claim," she announced. "Right beside yours."

Abe felt his heart give an extra thump, then sat down

on some clean rocks. He patted the rocks beside him. "Come, sit down. I need to talk to you."

She complied, then looked into his eyes. "Sounds serious."

He shook his head. "It's a serious subject, but that doesn't mean bad. In fact, it's good. The nicest thing I've thought about for a long time. No, it's the nicest thing I've thought about. . .ever." He stopped for breath hoping she'd say something to help him but she didn't.

"I've kinda grown used to you in the last little while," he started out. He stopped. That sounded like getting used to new shoes. Maybe shoes that hurt his feet at first. He'd better tell her how he felt about her or she'd never accept him.

He cleared his throat and started over again. "I mean, Miss Lawford, that I. . .do I have to keep calling you Miss Lawford forever? What's wrong with Martha and Abe?"

She giggled and tossed a small rock. "Martha and Abe are good. I like them just fine." The rock disappeared into a deep pool, sending out ripples to both banks.

Hope spread through his chest like the ripples from the stone. Maybe this wouldn't be so hard after all. He'd just spit out the plain words and see how she took them. He cleared his throat again. What if she said no? What if she hated the thought of it? What if she hated him?

Well, he'd never know until he asked. He pulled in an extra deep breath and rubbed a shiny circle on a round, whitish stone. "I've been thinking about you a lot lately," he finally managed. "I've been wondering. . .I've been . . .what are you planning to eat now that your food is gone and your buffalo chips, too?" As soon as the words left his mouth he hated himself for them. That could completely cloud the issue. He wasn't asking her to marry him because she was going to starve. He loved her and wanted to care for her the rest of their lives.

Her ivory complexion lightened almost to white, and she shook her head slowly. Picking up a head of dry grass, she tossed it into the water. After a time that seemed forever, her brilliant eyes met his. After a serious moment, she smiled and a twinkle crept back into her eyes. "I guess I'm going out somewhere and starve to death. Josie will go with me. She's hungrier and skinnier and weaker than I am." She reached both hands behind her and leaned on them, thinking. "Truly what am I going to do? I don't know. My uncle and aunt are way, way overdue. Maybe they'll come this afternoon."

Abe wanted to lay his large brown hand over her small white one, on the smooth rock. But he resisted the temptation. "You can't spend your life watching down the Trail for your kinfolks." He wiped the sweat from his forehead, knowing the day wasn't that warm. This was the time for him to ask her, but he didn't want her to think his proposal came from sympathy. *Good going, Noble. You just demolished the most important moment of your life.* He raised his eyes to find her looking at him with a question mark in hers.

"Martha," he spluttered. Then he rushed on before he had a chance to think up any more stupid ideas. "I want to marry you," he gushed so quickly she probably couldn't even understand his words.

eleven

Martha couldn't believe her ears. It had sounded as though Abe wanted to marry her! She watched a large brown bird, probably an eagle, circling in the clear blue sky above them. Abram Noble would never ask her to marry him! Never! Yes, she'd misunderstood his garbled words. She met his eyes. "I'm sorry," she said softly. "I'm afraid I didn't hear your last words."

Mr. Noble sighed then hesitated, as though unable to repeat it. Terror shot through Martha's veins like boiling water. He had! She'd heard him right the first time. He'd asked her to marry him!

"Uh, I asked you to marry me," he mumbled again. He jerked in a quick breath and went on. "I love you, Miss . . .I love you, Martha. I've loved you since I first laid eyes on you. Marry me and we'll build a house right here on the creek."

For some reason, she had to struggle for each breath. She'd never known a nicer man in her life, and she purely liked Abram Noble a whole lot. But she'd read lots of books. When she fell in love, she expected to see fireworks, hear bells ring, trumpets blare, flutes trill; then she'd feel a pink cloud wrap tightly around her. But right now she heard only a donkey braying down the street, and saw a puff of dust blowing across the creek.

Finally, she lifted her eyes to discover his kindly brown ones staring at her, apprehension etched in his entire face. How could she hurt him? He'd been so good to her. "I'm so shocked I don't know what to say," she whispered. "I had no idea. I had no idea at all. Could I have a little while to think about it?"

A small degree of relief relaxed his face. "Sure. You think as long as you want." He struggled to his feet and gave her a hand up. Neither said a word as they strolled back to her wagon; both hearts were too full.

As they reached their destination, he turned to leave. "See you later," he said in a muted voice as he walked off.

Martha dropped heavily to one of the dynamite boxes. Josie crowded against Martha, leaning her big head in Martha's lap. "What do you think of that?" Martha asked the big dog. She waited a moment then went on. "There never was a nicer man. But I have to be in love before I marry, so don't go getting excited about it." She sat staring off into the blue, wondering how she could tell him without hurting him, her hands idly caressing Josie's rough fur.

Then an entire new line of thought came to her. If she married Mr. Noble she wouldn't have a thing to worry about anymore. She'd have plenty to eat, a nice home. Josie would have enough to eat, too, the first time in a long time. She'd probably have a horse of her own . . . Sampson. As she thought about it she realized that Mr. Noble had no doubt bought Sampson mostly for her. Oh, what a nice man!

But she didn't love him! She'd read books about girls that married men for their money. She'd never do that to any man but especially not to Mr. . . . Abe. He was too fine a man to treat that way. *Oh, Lord,* she cried silently, *help me tell him without hurting him. I know you wouldn't want me to marry him for convenience, and I don't want to. But Lord, I'm in about as bad a position as a girl can get into. You know of course, but I'll tell You anyway. I don't have any food or fire to cook it with if I had it. Won't You help me get something to eat? Thank You, in Jesus' Name. Amen.*

After praying, she felt really hungry. Before, she'd been able to put it from her mind somehow, but now her stomach rumbled and she felt ravenous. Almost instantly she thought of the gun in the wagon. She didn't know how to shoot it but maybe she could learn. But, if she managed to kill something, how would she cook it? Her eyes fell on the myriad of large weeds surrounding her. Maybe they'd burn! She laughed. They'd probably burn like paper and be gone almost instantly.

Well, she might as well give it a try. Dragging the gun from the wagon, she sat down on a box and examined it. She had to put a shell in it but had no idea where. After looking at it for a while, she put it back in the wagon. She'd never figure it out alone. Maybe she could go ahead and gather up some of the weeds and see how they burned.

Show me what to do, Lord. Thank You for caring for Josie and me. Before she said "Amen," she saw a figure coming toward the wagon. Nellie Martin! And she held something in her hand. "Thank You, Lord," she said aloud. "I know You've answered my need as soon as I asked." She hurried to meet Nellie. "Hello," she called. "You don't know how glad I am to see you."

Nellie took a couple of skips and held out a brown package. "Mama made a loaf of bread for you," she said. "It's still warm, and she even sent some butter. I hope you're hungry."

"Oh, Nellie, you just don't know." When Martha took the bread, the smell made her so hungry she plopped down on a box, feeling weak. She'd been wishing Nellie would come see her again, but suddenly she desperately wanted her friend to leave so she could eat. She felt so hungry her legs actually shook. Then her eyes fell on Josie and her heart fell. The dog could eat the whole loaf in two gulps and still be hungry.

Nellie's voice brought Martha back. "I have to go back now, but I'll come see you tomorrow if that's all right."

Martha nodded, clutching the aromatic package in her hands. "Yes, come back, Nellie. We can take another walk."

Nellie barely turned away when Abe arrived, a rabbit in his hands. "I got a rabbit for Josie," he said, laying it in front of the skinny dog, who snatched it into her teeth and ran under the wagon with it. "Sorry I didn't find any firewood. I will though by tomorrow." He left immediately, too.

Finally, at long last, Martha pulled the golden loaf of bread from the brown paper. A loaf of real bread! It looked as good as it smelled. She'd had her last real bread the first few days after they had left Independence six months ago.

"Thank You, Lord," she said out loud. "I've never been more thankful than I am now, and You provided for both Josie and me almost before I asked. Thank You again. Amen." She tore the end off the bread and took a big bite without waiting to spread the butter. It tasted like manna from God. And it was.

Sinking onto the box, she concentrated on eating slowly. If she didn't, she'd eat the whole loaf without a thought for tomorrow, just like Josie. When she finished the first piece, she forced herself to put butter on the next one, and the next. When she'd eaten almost half the loaf, she wrapped it back up in the brown paper, even though she wanted more in the worst way. Would she ever again have all the food she wanted?

Josie chose that time to come out from under the wagon, licking her lips. The dog hadn't saved any for tomorrow, Martha noticed. When her pet started sniffing toward the brown paper, Martha took it into the wagon and put it inside the trunk. That bread would at least be a few bites for them tomorrow.

ð

Later, when she lay on her featherbed, she thought about Abe's kind offer of marriage. It would be so nice to have someone to care for her, to know she'd have plenty of food every day, and a warm dry place to sleep. It wasn't as if Mr. Noble. . .Abe were mean or unkind. He wasn't. He'd even thought of Josie tonight when Martha couldn't cook.

Wait! He brought food for Josie at almost the time Mrs. Martin sent Nellie with food for her. Could that have been coincidence? Hardly! Mr. Noble had arranged it all. Yes, no doubt about it. She looked skyward and folded her hands. "Lord, is Abe my raven? I know You're sending me food through him as You did Elijah through the ravens. Thank You, God. And thank You for Abe. I've never met a nicer person, Lord. Do You think I should go ahead and marry him?" She almost felt she should.

Then she remembered. They could get 320 acres! Twice as much as either could get alone. Besides that, the land would probably all be claimed before she turned twenty-one. Yes, she'd better forget her silly romantic ideas and get on with life the best way she knew. But she couldn't do it. That would be the meanest trick in the world to play on Abe.

❧

Early the next morning, she awakened to find frost on the ground. She took her morning sponge bath in cold water. Brrrr. It had been so much nicer when she could heat the water. She pulled on a clean brown dress that looked as if she'd walked across the country in it. She giggled because that's exactly what she'd done.

"Shall we divide the bread now or wait?" she asked Josie. The plumy tail wagged several times.

Before Martha could decide, Abe brought another loaf of bread, warm from the oven as the last one had been. Josie sniffed and grew restless.

Abe sat on one of the dynamite boxes and looked at her in a strange way. "Will you marry me, my little Martha? I'll be so good to you and care for you and love you with all my heart."

She couldn't do it. She owed him too much to hurt him by pretending something she didn't feel. Through almost unbearable pain, she shook her head. "I'm sorry, Mr. Noble. . .Abe. Josie, get back from this bread. I owe my very life to you and, more than words can say, I appreciate what you've done. But I would only hurt you if I married you, because although I consider you the best friend I've ever had, and purely know you're the kindest man I've ever met and I respect you more than anyone I've ever known, I don't love you as a woman should love a man she marries."

He flinched as if she'd given him a hard right to the chin and then he sort of wilted into a crumpled heap. He didn't say a word nor did he move. He just sat there, leaning forward, his elbows on his knees.

Seeing the pain in his eyes, Martha leaned over and put her hand on his arm. "I'm so sorry," she said. "I almost said yes, but I realized I'd be marrying you for the wrong reasons and that I'd hurt you more if I married you than if I didn't." She pushed back Josie's inquisitive face from the warm bread she still held. "You're a true friend, Abe, and it's hard for friends to hurt each other."

He shuddered and stood to his feet, smiling down at her. "It's all right. I had no reason to believe you cared for me. I—"

"Oh, but I do care for you, Mr. . . .Abe. I care for you very, very much, as a dear friend."

He smiled again, a tight smile that came out almost a grimace. "It's all right, Miss Lawford, don't give it another thought. I'll probably see you tomorrow." That was it. He rushed down the street without a backward look, his shoulders hunched.

Somehow, Martha no longer felt hungry for the bread she held in her lap. Josie had been trying to get her attention ever since Mr. . . .Abe had given her the bread. "Come on, Josie," Martha said wearily, "I'll get you the rest of yesterday's loaf." She patted the faithful head and climbed into the wagon to exchange the new loaf for the old. When she climbed down, she held out the bread. "You need it more than I do," she said.

She sat back on the dynamite box, watching Josie eat the bread in three quick bites, chewing each only a few times. "Well, our problems are still alive and healthy," she told the dog. "We still don't know where our next meal is coming from. . .and it's getting colder every night."

twelve

As Abe walked back to his boardinghouse, he decided he knew how a bullet in his heart would feel. He'd never known such pain in his life. Could he live without Martha? Would he actually die from the pain as he would a bullet?

He rushed straight to his room, avoiding talking to or even meeting anyone. Easing down to his bed, he closed his eyes. "I tried, God," he prayed aloud. "Is this the way You want it? How long will I hurt. . .forever? I don't think I can handle this that long." He rested a few moments while a single tear ran from his right eye, across his cheek, past his ear, and onto the coarse muslin sheet. "She'd starve if I didn't take her food. I'm not sure I can stand the pain of seeing her. But You know I can't let her get too hungry." He lay quietly thinking for a while. And the pain continued. "Could You just take away the pain, God? I'd be thanking You a long time if You'd just do that for me." But the pain continued.

He fell asleep. When he awakened, his mouth tasted awful and he felt blacker than his shaded room. How could he live in the same world with Martha and not be able to call her his own? He pushed open the faded denim curtains to find the sun had moved into the western sky. Abe had the distinct feeling God had been talking to him while he slept. He sat up and thought hard, unable to remember.

Dropping his feet to the floor, he tried to think but couldn't get past his pain. He grabbed his hat and jacket and went out to check on the horses. Even though the sun still shone most of the time on these early November days, it didn't have enough strength to warm the air much.

When Charity saw him coming, she nickered and trotted to the fence. Sampson followed, almost reluctantly. "You're my best girl, aren't you?" Abe said to the horse, rubbing her neck and shoulders. Sampson shoved his big head against Abe's hand. "Oh, you want some, too, eh?" Abe said, pleased to know the big horse was beginning to care.

Abe gave both horses some oats and headed for the saloon.

"Heard about Slick?" the barkeep asked when Abe settled onto the stool.

Abe shook his head, reaching for the coffee he'd been served. He'd forgotten all about Slick. The man might be dead—small loss.

"Well, he got beat up the other night," the barkeep announced. "Someone hauled him out to Fort Walla Walla, more dead than alive. But I hear he's about well now. Purty hard to get rid of a skunk like that."

So, the old geezer lived. Abe couldn't tell whether he felt relief or disappointment. His own intense pain crowded out all other emotions.

Abe ate a roast meat sandwich without tasting it, then wondered what Martha had eaten that day. Sure would be a lot easier to feed her if the poor dog wasn't always twice as hungry. After ordering another sandwich wrapped, he hurried to the meat shop where he ordered a rabbit. Upon being told the rabbit was for a dog, the butcher offered him a bunch of meat scraps at no charge, adding that he could pick up scraps every day.

Abe, carrying the sandwich in one hand and the big bag

of scraps in the other, headed for Martha and Josie. He straightened his shoulders. He'd act as if he'd forgotten all about the proposal and rejection. He'd just be a casual friend again. *But how could he do that?* He just would, that's all there was to it. He would.

She walked to meet him, a worried look on her face. But why should she feel bad? She's the one who'd said no. He forced a big smile to his lips. "I just learned you can get free meat scraps for Josie every day at the meat shop," he said in a superficially cheerful voice. He handed her the sandwich and dumped the scraps onto the grassy ground for Josie, who snatched up a meaty bone and retreated to her special spot under the wagon.

"Come sit down for a while," she invited.

He complied. "Have you been noticing how cold it's getting at night? Not too warm in the daytime, either."

She nodded. "I know I can't live in the wagon all winter. Thankfully my uncle and aunt are coming. I've been having a feeling it will be real soon."

He nodded. "It better be." He pointed east at the bluish, snow-capped mountains. "Have you noticed we get new snow in the Blues about once a week now? They may be impassable already and it's going to get worse in a hurry."

"I know. They'll be here soon," she said with a weak giggle. "I just have a feeling in my bones it'll be soon." She swallowed. "I guess I'm not very grown-up, not being able to care for myself and all," she added in a tight murmur.

"It's hard for a woman," he said. "How can a woman earn money here? The only possibility I see would be working in one of the saloons, and you let me know you weren't interested in that."

She hung her head, her face pink. "But I did try," she whispered as if confessing to something indecent. "I tried both of them and they said no." She sniffed. "I tried all the businesses. No one wanted me."

He felt another stab. This time for her pain. She'd tried her best, done everything she could, and still she sat here helpless and hopeless. He draped another smile across his face. "Good thing your kinfolks are coming soon," he said, getting up. "I better be getting back. Mrs. Martin wants her guests to be on time for supper. Guess I don't blame her much." He took a few steps and turned back. "You eat that sandwich yourself, see? Josie still has some meat scraps." He smiled a genuine smile. "How long has it been since she walked off and left food?"

Martha laughed softly and shook her head. "I can't even remember. Thanks, Abe, you're the best friend I ever had. Josie, too."

❧

He hurried to his room where he washed up, then rushed on to the dining room.

"You ain't looking so good," Nellie said when she sat down across the table from him.

"I'm all right, Nellie, just hungry." He didn't feel hungry at all but had already made up his mind to eat all he could force down to keep up his strength.

When he finished eating, he went out to see the horses again. "I should take each of you out for a ride," he told them, "but I don't seem to have the hankering right now." He lumbered back to his room and flopped down onto his bed. Martha didn't look any happier than he felt. Well, she had plenty of problems, even if a broken heart wasn't among them. How would it feel to be a girl in this country with nothing, not even food, and unable to find work?

It would be awful, no doubt, but would it hurt as bad as what was hurting him? Finally, he shook his head. Probably as bad but different.

Abe, I want you to marry her.

"I tried, God," he cried out loud. "You heard me. What are You talking about?"

Your broken heart will heal when you stop feeling sorry for yourself and think of her problems. Marry her. You can save her the pain she's enduring now.

"Do You have it all figured out how I can do that, God, since she doesn't want me?"

I do. Now you figure it out and marry her.

That stopped Abe. Completely stopped him. How do you marry someone when she tells you in plain words she doesn't love you?

Suddenly, he had a feeling he should take the horses out for a ride. Getting up from the bed, he shoved his hat onto his head, put on his jacket again, and headed for the corral. Both horses greeted him eagerly this time. "Should I saddle you both or ride you, Charity, and lead Sampson?" The horses both danced eagerly and followed him on the other side of the fence until he went into the room referred to as the tack room. He saddled both horses, hopped up into Charity's saddle, and, with Sampson's reins in his left hand, headed west. He'd just give them a little run before it got dark.

Before he realized it, he found himself approaching Martha's covered wagon. He started to rein Charity south but then he thought, why not, and moved up to the wagon and stopped the horses. "Anyone home?" he called. "Quiet," he said softly to the eagerly prancing horses who weren't ready to stop.

Her dark head appeared between the dirty white

curtains of the top of the wagon, then she hopped down.

"Want to take a little ride?" he asked. "The horses are needing some exercise."

"I'd enjoy that. Just let me get a coat." A moment later, she appeared, wrapped in a man's coat many sizes too large. "Don't laugh," she said. "This was Papa's coat. I don't have anything warm except blankets."

His heart felt a new pain. She didn't have warm clothes, living out here in the cold. "Come on, your horse can't wait."

After helping her mount, he climbed aboard Charity, and they headed southeast.

He noticed several new rough buildings. "Where do they all come from?" Martha asked, almost reading his mind.

"People are drifting in from all over, now that the Indian wars are over and the area's opened up for settling. I predict this place will look totally different a year from now." He swept his arm over the panoramic scene before them. "People and houses will be everywhere." Charity could hardly handle walking, and Sampson didn't do much better. Both horses added many quick steps to the slow pace. Abe reined Charity in. Martha did the same with Sampson. Abe looked down at Josie, dashing around, sniffing all the smells. He pointed a thumb at the dog. "Think we could give the horses a little run? Maybe we could tie her up for a while?"

Martha thought a moment. "Let's give the horses their head for a little while. If she falls behind, maybe she'll wait." She shrugged and gave him a smile that turned his stomach inside out. "I don't think I could tie her. It would break her heart."

Abe wouldn't push. He knew all about broken hearts.

He touched Charity with his heels. "Come on, girl, let's give that big loafer something to complain about." She stretched into a long lope and, with Martha's experienced guidance, Sampson stayed at her side. Abe glanced back for Josie who hadn't given up yet. She tore along beside Sampson, her tongue hanging out the side of her mouth. As he watched she slowed, and the hurt in her eyes seemed to match that hurt burning a hole in his heart. He pulled the slack from the reins. "Sorry, girl," he said quietly, "we can't leave our faithful buddy behind." Josie's grateful eyes told him thank you. The dog dropped to the grass, panting hard.

A moment later, Martha and Sampson returned. "Anything wrong?" she asked.

Abe pointed to the dog. "That dog would run until she dropped," he said. "I don't run horses too hard and I guess that goes for dogs, too. Why don't you and Sampson go on and have a good time? Then you can stay with Josie while Charity and I take a run."

ƨ

An hour later, he told Martha goodbye amidst her sincere thanks. He took his time rubbing the horses down, then gave them some hay and carried thirteen buckets of fresh water from the creek for their tank.

Sometime after he fell asleep, he awakened, feeling that Someone had been talking to him. He knew now what he had to do. He had to get Martha to agree to marry him in name only. In name only! Now, how could a man marry a woman like Martha in name only? Every minute he spent with her he longed to hold her in his arms and love and kiss her. He could do that—marry her in name only— if he didn't love her so much. Things being as they were, that foolish thought was out. Completely out! He dropped his head back onto the pillow and fell asleep.

When he awakened again, darkness still filled his bedroom and he felt as if Someone had spoken to him another time. Oh, no! He had to marry Martha—in name only!

All right, just for the sake of argument, say he did marry her. How would that be accomplished? He knew! He knew all the answers! He'd simply build the house exactly on the line between her 160 acres and his. And the house would be built with a bedroom on each end with the living area between. And he wouldn't set foot past the living area. Never! Not once!

He sat up again. "God," he called, "are You doing this to me, or am I having an awful nightmare?"

I'm here, Abe. You can do it. Then you'll be blessed as my first Abram was. You'll have more cattle than you can count. You'll be rich in worldly goods as well as heavenly.

"Look, God, You made me the way I am. I won't be able to stay in my end of the house and You know it. I'll mess this up something fierce. Then what?"

You won't mess it up. You'll keep your promise one hundred and ten percent, Abram. You can and you will. You have more strength than you realize.

Abe jumped from his bed and marched around the room several times. Maybe if he thoroughly awakened himself, the dream would be gone for good. He sure didn't want it returning again. Twice was more than enough. Finally, thoroughly chilled, he tumbled back into his bed.

thirteen

Martha awakened in the night, shivering. Every blanket she owned already lay over her. "Come closer, Josie," she whispered into the darkness. Josie didn't move so Martha leaned over and began tugging on the dog who, upon understanding the invitation, gladly crawled into the warm nest. Martha pulled Josie's rug atop the pile of blankets. That should do it.

She felt warmer, whether from the dog or the old rug or both, she didn't care. Cold was a totally miserable feeling. She soon fell asleep, her arms wrapped tightly around the elated dog.

It seemed she scarcely closed her eyes when Josie piled out of the bed and also the wagon. The sun shone brightly. Somebody must be coming, otherwise Josie would have been happy to cuddle until the sun warmed them a little. Martha pulled the blankets over herself for another moment. She simply hated getting out of bed these cold mornings. In a moment, she threw the covers back and hopped out, gritted her teeth, and poured some water into her wash bowl. For the first time ice chips edged the bucket of water. She almost cried out at the touch of the water, but she continued to wash herself. One thing that didn't cost money was cleanliness and she'd be clean. Even if it killed her.

Josie stood, looking south. Martha looked for a long time but didn't see anything. "Nothing there, Josie," she said. She looked at Josie's meat and saw several pieces left. Climbing into the wagon, she pulled the remaining loaf of bread from the trunk. Some good food would probably warm them both up. Spreading half of the butter liberally on half the bread, she put the other half of the loaf back into the trunk so it wouldn't tempt either her or Josie. After giving Josie her half, Martha sat down on a dynamite box. "Thank You, Father," she said, "not only for the food but for loving me so much. I love You too, Father." She ate her bread, taking tiny bites and chewing until the bread turned to liquid in her mouth. When the last crumb disappeared, she called Josie to take a walk to the creek for water.

Ten minutes later, she found herself standing beside Mill Creek on the property Abe planned to claim. She pivoted in a complete circle. What a beautiful world! Warm sunshine everywhere and bright blue sky in the west. Fresh snow covered the top third of the Blue Mountains, making them look like blueberry ice cream covered with whipped cream. Then a black shadow darkened her world. What about her uncle and aunt? Her cousin and brother? They *had* to get over those mountains before they became impassable. They simply had to.

Her happiness gone, she scooped up the bucket of water and carried it back to the wagon.

Abe waited for them, sitting on one of the boxes. He had another loaf of bread and a bowl of butter. Martha's heart swelled almost to bursting with gratitude. She'd spurned his generous offer of marriage and here he was, faithfully bringing her food—her raven from God.

Then she noticed his face. "You look as if you didn't get much sleep last night," she said. "I hope you weren't cold."

"No, I wasn't cold." He gave her the bread. "Would you like for me to leave so you can eat?"

She shook her head. "We ate before we went after water. I don't know how to thank you, Abe. You're definitely the kindest man in the world." She climbed into the wagon to put the bread into the trunk.

He still sat on the box, looking at her in a strange way. What was he thinking? Was her hair coming out? He definitely had something on his mind. She sat down on the other box and waited for him to speak his thoughts.

"I still want to marry you."

Oh, no. She thought she'd made her feelings clear. She couldn't find any words. She simply shook her head slowly.

"Don't say anything until I explain. I already know that you think I'm a great friend, so that's what we'll be. We'll get our three hundred twenty acres and build our house right on the line, yours on the east and mine on the west." He chuckled softly. "Or vice versa if you prefer. The house will have a bedroom at each end with the living area in between. Neither one of us will set foot on the other's private territory. We'll work together turning the place into a farm and ranch, dividing the profits in half." He stopped for a moment, watching her. "You can see, we'll both be better off with the arrangement, can't you?" he asked as if any fool could see the wisdom of his plan.

"You stayed up all night figuring this out, didn't you?" she finally asked.

He barked out a hoarse laugh. "I guess you might say I did just that."

She sat silent for a moment, thinking. She could see how a plan like this would work between friends, but he'd said he loved her. "The arrangement still wouldn't be fair to you," she finally said. "You said you. . .you said you . . .uh. . . ."

"I said I loved you? Why don't you just forget that? I

have." He grinned and snapped his fingers. "It's all over, just like that." His face became serious again. "I don't mean to push, but you have to do something right away. One morning you're going to wake up and have to shovel your way out of the wagon."

"You're the nicest person in the entire world."

His eyes brightened. "But you still don't love me?"

"I do love you, a whole lot. You're the best friend I've ever had."

He slumped a tiny bit. "All right, I'll never mention it to you again. From here on out, we're best friends. How's that?"

Martha laughed out loud. "Good."

"Then you'll marry me?"

"I don't know about that. I just don't know, Abe. Marriage is forever and that's a long time."

Suddenly, Josie began to bark and Martha followed her gaze south. Covered wagons! A whole line of covered wagons! She pointed and Abe looked, too. They must have been five miles away but winding toward them.

"That's my aunt and uncle!" she shouted. "They're finally here. Abe, they're almost here!" She felt like grabbing him and dancing right off to meet the wagons. She should make them a big meal! Then she flopped back to earth. They were much too far to run to meet yet—she didn't have a thing to feed them. Maybe they'd have something for her.

Abe smiled. "Well, I guess they got through the Blues. I'm glad for you, Martha. I guess you won't be needing me anymore." He got up and stretched.

She pushed him back onto the dynamite box. "You're not going anywhere, Abram Noble. You just sit right there and meet my kin." She shivered with delight. "Oh, Abe, my brother's with them. You'll get to meet Jackson!"

She simply couldn't sit still. She jumped up and walked around the wagon, came back and sat down, then jumped up again. Finally, she held her hand to him. "Come on, let's go meet them. I can't sit here and wait."

He laughed but got up. "They're two or three hours away, Martha, by wagon or foot. If Josie would stay here we could take the horses and meet them in less than an hour. The horses would like that."

"Let's get the horses, Abe. I have to see my family! I can't wait one hour, let alone three."

Abe looked at Josie. "What about her, Martha? Since you're getting meat scraps for her she's strengthening, but she can't go that far. Are you willing to tie her up?"

Martha met Josie's sad brown eyes. The plumy tail wagged twice over the dog's back. It seemed as if the big dog understood their conversation. Could she do that to Josie? Her excitement waned some. "I don't have a rope," she said.

"I do. Want me to get it? And the horses?"

Martha vacillated. She simply had to see her family. She couldn't desert her faithful dog, and Josie really couldn't run all that way. Her eyes met Abe's. "What should we do?"

"I'll get her some more scraps to eat while we're gone. It won't hurt her a bit." He took off toward the meat market, returning shortly with a big bag of bloody scraps. "Don't let her have any now," he said, trotting off toward the horses' corral.

Ten minutes later, he came back astride Charity, leading Sampson and swinging a long rope as if it were a lariat. Jumping to the ground, he fastened one end of the rope to the wagon tongue so Josie could get on either side or under the wagon. "Bring the meat over," he said, "and let's make our getaway while she's eating."

Martha ran to Sampson's side, put her left foot into the stirrup, swung up, and adjusted her skirts so she felt modest.

"Let's go," Abe said, taking off in the general direction of the wagon train. The horses, eager for a good run, stretched into smooth gallops.

Martha felt a tremendous exhilaration. Although she'd learned to love Sampson a lot and thrilled in his long comfortable gait, her excitement came from knowing that in a little while she'd be reunited with her uncle, aunt, cousin, and brother. "I just can't believe it's all over," she called to Abe, only about twenty feet away on Charity.

After some time, Abe reined Charity in to a trot. Sampson slowed, too. "They haven't had much exercise lately," he explained at her questioning look. He grinned. "After a while we'll let them go again if they want." The wagon train still looked a long way off, maybe miles for all she knew.

They walked the horses and talked quietly. Martha noticed neither mentioned the terribly important subject they'd been discussing when they'd discovered the wagon train. What's more, she didn't know whether she'd marry him or not. He might withdraw the offer anyway, now that she had her kinfolk.

"Exciting, isn't it?" His smile looked tired. "Your life will undergo a quick and definite change now."

She nodded. One way or the other it would. If she married Abe it would. If she lived with her kin it would change, too. Oh, why didn't the wagon train hurry? Or why didn't *they*? "Abe, if we don't let the horses run some more, I'm getting off and run myself."

He grinned. "I think they're rested." He nudged Charity with his knees. "Want to go again, girl?" The horse took off at full speed. Sampson fell behind but soon caught her.

Martha felt the exhilaration again. "They really like to

run, don't they?"

"I see you do, too," he returned.

This time Abe let Charity go until they met the first wagon. "Hello there," he called, turning Charity to walk beside the man, going north now, back the way they'd come. "You headed for Steptoeville?"

"Walla Walla," the man answered.

Abe nodded. "Steptoeville's in Walla Walla County," he said, pointing north. "Dead ahead."

Martha sat quietly on Sampson as long as she could. Finally, she cleared her throat so only Abe could hear.

"Could you direct us to the Strange wagon?" Abe asked.

The man grinned. "All our wagons are strange," he said as if joining in a joke.

Abe laughed. "I mean the Cleveland Strange wagon." He motioned to Martha. "This is Martha Lawford, and they're her kinfolk. Her brother, Jackson, is with them."

The man wrinkled his forehead. "Nobody on this train named Strange," he finally said. "Everybody'd of knowed 'em with that name." He thought a moment then shook his head. "No Lawfords, neither."

Martha couldn't keep quiet any longer. "They have to be on this train, sir. I got here about a month ago, and they were on the next train. I know they're here." A big lump formed in her stomach. "I'm going to check every wagon."

Abe came to her. "Want me to come with you?"

Unable to speak, she nodded.

She did exactly as she'd said, asking at every single wagon. No one had so much as heard of anyone named Strange or Lawford. When she'd questioned the last wagon, she nudged Sampson with her heels, flew several hundred feet away from the train, reined in, slid from the saddle, and dropped onto the ground, unable to support her own weight.

fourteen

Martha'd barely fallen to the ground, still holding Sampson's reins in her hand, when she heard Charity arrive, then felt strong arms surrounding her.

"I'm sorry, Martha," Abe said. "I wish your family had been there." He held her close, patting her back. "I'm sorry. I'm so sorry," he kept murmuring against her hair. In the background she heard the wagons creaking, oxen bawling, children crying, people yelling, all the sounds she'd listened to for six long months. The sounds along with the knowledge that she had no one, made her physically ill. Jumping from Abe's arms, she handed him Sampson's reins, ran about thirty feet away, pulled her skirts back, leaned over, and retched until she had nothing in her stomach.

She straightened her skirts, took several deep breaths, and scolded herself for being immature. Her eyes swept east until she found Abe, sitting where she'd left him. When their eyes met, he jumped to his feet and trotted to her. She met him halfway. "Thank you for leaving me alone while I acted the part of a baby," she whispered.

He shook his head briskly. "You're no baby. Anyone would be upset." For a full minute he stood on one foot then the other watching her closely. "Ready to head back?"

"Might as well." The wagon train had moved a little ahead of them. "Did you ask where they're headed?"

"Yes. They're headed for donation claims in Steptoeville."

"Did you ask if there were any trains behind them?"

He shook his head. "Why don't we ask them, then give the horses their heads. We'll get home long before the train arrives."

"No one else is goin' through those mountains till the snow melts," the man replied to Abe's questions. "If I had it to do over again I'd wait at Fort Hall until spring. We like ta kilt our oxen goin' up and almost lost our wagons comin' down. Snow's two feet deep up there already."

Martha's last hope plummeted with the man's words. As Sampson plodded along and Abe talked to the man, she remembered her situation—not a bite of food for her or Josie, no way she could think of to get any, and the cold weather upon her.

Abe caught up with her. "I guess you heard."

She nodded.

"Let's get back to Josie." He touched Charity with his foot, and she stretched out in long smooth strides with Sampson moving alongside.

The horses raced most of the way back, slowing to a trot once for fifteen minutes. When they stopped beside the wagon, Josie greeted Martha as though they'd been apart for three months. Sitting on the dried grass, Martha let the dog wallow over her, realizing Josie was all she had now. As Josie crowded close, licking her hands, she gave the dog lots of hugs and pats.

Abe said nothing as he sat on a dynamite box watching the emotional greetings. Finally, Martha managed to get her feet under her. Josie shoved her body against Martha and tried to get to her face, obviously not finished with the greeting. "That's enough, Josie," Martha said in a flat voice. "Lie down." With a long sad look, the dog crumpled beside Abe. When Martha sat on the other box, Josie crept over to lie beside her.

No one said anything for some time. Martha wanted to but she couldn't think of a thing. At this point she felt empty, as though she had no beginning and no end. And she didn't care what happened. But when her eyes fell on the dog at her feet, she discovered she did care. She owed Josie. She owed her a good home and enough food.

"What you thinking about?" Abe's soft voice asked. "Or dare I ask?"

Her eyes met his and the care she saw made her smile. "You can ask anything you want, Abe. I'm sure you have a good idea what I was thinking."

He wrapped his tanned hands together. "You were deciding to marry me?"

Martha almost jumped. That was the one thing she hadn't been thinking about. "I'm not sure what I was thinking," she said, "but here's what crossed my mind just now. Do you think Josie and I should try to get to The Dalles? There might be some work I could do there."

His eyes opened wide. "Why would you think about that? Does marrying me sound that awful? Anyway, I doubt you could get there until spring. There won't be much traffic this winter."

He got up. "I'm going now. You'll have to decide your own fate. If I could, I'd stir up your brain a little." He walked over to Charity and got on her, then turned back to Martha. "I'll be around." He took off toward the back of the boardinghouse with Sampson in tow.

❧

When Abe disappeared from Martha's sight, she felt totally alone. She turned her attention to Josie. "And now it's just you and me," she said. "We could go get you some bones but Abe already did that. Are you hungry for some bread?" Making no move to get the bread, her mind sped in circles. Abe still wanted to marry her.

If she refused, he'd keep bringing food to her but how fair was that to him? Besides, she had to get out of the wagon and soon. It could snow at any time. She could feel it in the night air lately. Where it had been fun living in the wagon when they first started west, and it hadn't been all that bad other than for the loneliness she felt when she got parked here, it was just plain miserable now.

She dropped to her knees beside the box. "You have to help me, Lord," she cried. "Would You want me to marry Abe for convenience? It seems to me that would be sacrilegious, making marriage vows that I wouldn't mean to keep. Show me, Lord. I'm at the end, the very end." She rested quietly on her knees for a while, then looked up toward the bright blue sky, halfway noticing the sun almost directly overhead. "Lord, You promised to be with us always and to hear our prayers. Well, where are my aunt and uncle? And my brother? It feels to me You've deserted me just as all my earthly kin have." She lowered her face to the box and let the tears flow freely. Josie inched as close as she could and licked Martha's cheeks where the tears rolled over them.

Martha felt desperately tired and crawled into the wagon to rest. Josie followed and snuggled close. They fell asleep together and awakened to a lot of commotion as the wagon train rolled to a stop a half-mile south.

Two young men on horses galloped to her wagon. "Any place to get supplies?" the older of the two asked Martha as she stepped down from her wagon.

She pointed toward the street. "There's a general store, two saloons, a boardinghouse, and a trader. I'm sure someone will be able to help."

The young man tipped his hat and turned his horse into the street. "Those places will always help if you have money," she told Josie. "Come on, let's go see Nellie."

Martha had never gone after Nellie but she needed someone to be with this afternoon.

☙

As they walked, Nellie took several quick peeks at Martha.
They reached Mill Creek and stopped to watch it gurgle
over the stones.

Nellie sat on the clean rocks and Martha followed. Josie
ran into the cold water, back and forth from side to side,
cavorting first in the water then the grass. "You've been
crying," Nellie said softly. "What's the matter, Martha?
Does it have something to do with the wagon train?"

Martha nodded. "Yes. I thought my kinfolk would be
with it, but they aren't. They say the snow is bad in the
Blues and no one else can. . .," she stopped and swallowed hard. The lump stayed in her throat so she swallowed twice more. "No one else can get through till
spring," she finally choked out. Leaning her head on her
hands, she swallowed again, her eyes shut tight.

Nellie put her arm over Martha's shoulders. "I'm sorry,"
she murmured into Martha's ear. "I'm really sorry. Have
you figured what you're going to do?"

Martha shook her head as it still rested in her hands.

"You could stay with me, but my sister sleeps with me
and the room is so tiny. My two other sisters have a tiny
room just like ours." She thought a moment. "I don't
know what Mama would say, but you can't spend the
winter in that wagon."

Martha didn't lift her head but her mind kept busy. She
wanted to tell Nellie about Abe's proposal but didn't know
whether it would be right. She didn't tell. After a few
minutes she lifted her head and smiled at Nellie. "Please,
don't worry about me. Your mother can't take in every
stray that comes along. If she did you'd all starve." She
giggled as she watched Josie wallowing in the grass on

the other side of the creek. "And she definitely wouldn't want Josie in her nice clean house." She giggled again as she thought about the rough boards from which the boardinghouse was built. Her farm house in Missouri had had hardwood floors with beautiful rugs on them.

Just at that time the big dog decided to share the nice cold water with the girls. Splashing up from the creek, she shook vigorously. Screaming, both girls jumped from their comfortable seats and ran back toward the wagon.

Nellie hurried back to the boardinghouse to help with supper, and Martha pulled out the fresh loaf of bread, tore it in half, put one half back, and shared the other half with Josie.

After she ate she crawled into the wagon to think. She couldn't think of any other way than to marry Abe. And it really didn't sound so bad. Especially the way he described it to her the last time. A business arrangement. She knew he'd keep his agreement, too. The more she thought about it the better it sounded. She'd have her 160 acres, too, right away. She'd have a house and a garden and all the food she and Josie needed. Thinking about Josie reminded her how kind Abe was. She could count on him to be good to Josie as well as her. She jumped down from the wagon. "Come on, Josie, let's go look at our homesite again."

They stayed for half an hour and came back. For some reason, Martha felt a little disappointed. Then she realized why. She'd hoped to meet Abe there—and that he'd beg her to marry him again.

They hadn't been back at the wagon long when Nellie came with a loaf of bread and some hot sliced meat. Martha's mouth watered at the smell and so did Josie's. She knew that God's raven, Abe, had arranged this fantastic meal. She asked Nellie.

Nellie colored. "I'm not sure. . .uh. . .I'm not supposed to tell." She looked at her friend. "You never asked before. I didn't think you would. Well, I'm not saying. My word is bound."

Martha gave her friend a little shove. "You told me already, Nellie. Can you tell him thanks for me?"

Nellie's red head waved back and forth. "Then he'd know I told." Nellie soon left and Josie let Martha know she was ready for her meal. "I wish I could cook your meat," she told the dog. "Then you'd know you had a meal." She started to go put the bread in the trunk and get the other loaf but changed her mind. "Let's have a real banquet," she told Josie. She wrapped a thin slice of meat in a big piece of bread and offered it to the dog, who swallowed it in one gulp.

Martha felt disappointed. "That's not fair," she told her pet. "Now you're going to want my piece, too." She broke off another piece of bread, tossed it under the wagon, and kicked several meaty bones over it. "Now you go eat and let me eat in peace," she told Josie who ran under and lay down to her meal.

Martha didn't eat slowly. In fact she tried to eat all she wanted while the dog busied herself with the things under the wagon. The bread and meat tasted better than anything she remembered, and she ate much of it. For the first time in months she felt stuffed.

After she finished, she waited in camp hoping Abe would come. She hoped he'd come and insist on marrying her. But he didn't come. She spent the longest evening of her life waiting and watching for the tall spare man to step from the boardinghouse and stride to the wagon.

fifteen

Abe dropped to his bed to think. He'd managed to force down a little food at supper though it had tasted like dried grass. He longed to run down to Martha at the wagon to see how she was now. After what she'd been through today she needed him. He knew full well she did. But something or Someone held him back as if it weren't the right thing to do.

By now he'd decided he'd be glad to marry her on any terms. Just to be near her and know she was all right. How could he ask for more? Yes, he'd go ask her again. He got up, put on his hat, and opened the door. But he shut it again and sat back on the bed. What was this, anyway?

As he sat there wondering why he'd come back, he saw clearly that she would feel pushed if he went to her now, that he'd have to be patient until she came to him. As that thought came, a peace fell over him, and he knew she would come. *Thank you, God*, he thought. *I should have known You were showing me what to do.* He pulled off his clothes, tumbled into bed, and fell into a sound sleep.

&

The next morning, he awakened feeling great. Pulling back his coarse denim curtains, he saw a cloudless blue sky. "God is in His heaven and all's right with the world," he said out loud. He opened his door, retrieved a pitcher of warm water, poured it into his wash bowl, and proceeded to give himself a good cleaning. After dressing, he poured the water into a large can in the hall and stepped outside.

Buttoning his jacket against the cold, he couldn't help glancing west. Martha and Josie moved around the wagon, but he couldn't tell what they were doing. Resolutely, he turned away and strode east down the street to the creek, then south, then east again as the creek made another turn. He followed the creek for about 200 feet and stopped. What a place for a claim! And they'd do it together. Somehow he'd been assured of it. They'd do it together, and he'd be satisfied just to be with her. He took off his hat and bowed his head. *Thank You, God,* he said silently. *You were right, it will be enough. And I can do it with Your help.* He replaced his hat and stood looking over the sun-drenched acres before him.

"Hello, Abe. Is this a private meeting? Or am I welcome?" Martha looked as happy as he felt this morning.

Abe couldn't believe the relief he felt at seeing her radiant smile. "Welcome, Martha. I was just looking the place over one more time. Guess I'll make my claim today before some of that new bunch on the wagon train gets it." He hadn't really thought about making his claim today but it sounded good. He walked a little ways up the creek. "Do you think I could ever be sorry if I made the claim here?" he asked.

"No. How could you, Abe? There's no prettier piece of land in Washington Territory."

He met her blue eyes. They reached right inside him, almost to his toes. "All right, I'll see you later," he said, turning to leave. *Who was driving him, anyway? He hadn't wanted to leave yet. After all, the whole day lay before him.* He strode off toward the street.

But her feet patted the soft ground until she caught up

with him. "Could we talk before you make your claim?"
she asked breathlessly.

He stopped. "Sure. Where?"

She looked back up the creek. "Back on the place? Or
we could go to the wagon."

Wordlessly, he turned and hurried back to where they'd
come from. "Want to sit on the creek bank?" he asked.
She sat. "Now," he said after they both got comfortable
and Josie disappeared up the creek someplace, "what did
you have in mind to talk about?"

She turned a rosy red under her faded blue sunbonnet.
"Whatever you'd like to talk about," she said quietly.

He wanted desperately to ask her again to marry him
but something held him back. He looked down at her and
his heart turned over in his chest. He shook his head. "I
don't have nothin' special in mind," he said. "You just
go ahead with whatever's botherin' you. Is something
wrong? Are you all right? I have to say you look good
this morning. I'm right proud of you after the disappointment you had yesterday."

She seemed to wilt, then straightened up, her shoulders
back. "Are you taking a claim for one hundred sixty
acres?" she finally asked.

He nodded. "That's the law, Martha. It's a fair bit more
land than I ever owned before."

"Would you like to have more?" she asked very quietly.

He laughed softly. "Most men want more no matter
what they got. Sure, I'd like more but I'd also be happy
with a lot less." He thought a moment. "Gotta get going
on it, too, so I can get a cabin built before it gets much
colder."

They sat together for several minutes, neither of them

talking, both thinking private thoughts. Josie came back with a small fish in her mouth. After giving a few pitiful twists, the fish quieted, and the dog swallowed it whole.

Finally, Martha met Abe's eyes again. "You know you could have more, don't you?"

He shook his head. "Not according to the present law."

Another long silence. *I know what she's doing, God. Why do I have to let her sit in such pain and embarrassment?* He didn't say anything more.

"What if we were to marry?" she asked almost in a whisper.

He almost sprang around to face her. "You want to? You want to marry me?" he asked.

She hung her head. "Well, you suggested something. Abe!" she said louder. "Don't you remember all the things we talked about? About a private room at each end of the house?"

He felt a small disappointment, then happiness. "Sure, I remember. Want to do it?"

"I want you to understand everything if we do, Abe. I'm in a terrible situation, and I can't think of any other way. If I don't marry you, you'll keep buying food for me and Josie, and that isn't fair, either. I can't think of any way that'll be fair to you, Abe, but if you want to marry me, you can at least have my 160 acres."

He shook his head. "No, Martha, we'll have 320 acres. The whole place will be ours, unless you want to keep it divided. . .like our bedrooms."

They sat in silence for several minutes, Abe wondering what she was thinking. All he wanted to do was get married—quickly and now.

Finally, she looked into his eyes again. "Who would do it?"

"Do what? Oh, you mean marry us. Well, there's the Catholic priest. He has that little pole building south of the street. You know, they just built it."

She thought a moment. "Oh, that shacky thing we step around when we come to the property."

"Yeah. And the Methodists just organized a church here. They don't have a building yet, but I'll bet they have a priest around somewhere."

She laughed. "Minister, Abe. Methodists don't have priests."

He laughed, too. "Could one of those fellows do the job?"

She fell silent again, drawing a line in the dust between two stones. "What if one of us gets tired of this arrangement?" she finally asked.

Was she thinking she might fall in love with someone else? That thought was too horrible to even consider. "I'm not plannin' to," he said. "Are you?"

She continued drawing the dusty line downward toward the creek. Then, shaking her dark head, she lifted her eyes to his. "It would more likely be you, Abe. I realize this arrangement isn't fair for you." Her eyes dipped to her finger in the dust as though it were the most important thing in the world. Then she giggled. "You'd have been a lot better off if you weren't so nice. Know that?"

He shook his head. "If I hadn't helped you I'd have missed out on the nicest, prettiest woman I've ever known." He stopped, hoping he hadn't said too much. "Well, shall we go find someone to hitch us? Then we can get our claim." He laughed out loud. "All 320 acres of it, Martha." He got to his feet and pulled her up. "Which man should we get, a Catholic? Or a Methodist?"

She hesitated. "I'd. . .uh. . .I'd rather have a civil ceremony seeing as how it isn't a real marriage, but I guess there's no one around to do it that way."

"We could ask the claims man," he said. "If he can't, then there's no one else around here to do a civil ceremony."

Abe led Martha to the trader's building where the claims people had an office in the back. "We was wondering if you could marry us," Abe said, embarrassed. "Then we want to take out a donation claim."

"Sorry," the short round man said. "You better let the priest or minister do that, then we'll talk about the claim."

Back outside, Abe met Martha's eyes. "Want to let the priest do it?" He hesitated with his next thought for he desperately wanted this marriage to be *until death do us part*. But in fairness to her he had to say it. "I hear a marriage can be annulled if it isn't consummated."

She raised her eyebrows in question, then shrugged. "Fine with me. Let's go."

They walked between the meat market and Galbraith's Saloon to the shack that people called a church. Without a doubt the poorest building in the settlement, the poles didn't begin to cover the walls. When they went inside, Abe saw lots of daylight through the roof and dirt made up the dusty floor. One shaky bench was the only furniture in sight.

"May I help you?" a man wearing a clerical collar over rough worn clothes asked with a noticeably French accent.

Abe cleared the clog from his throat. "I hope so, Father. The young woman and I wish to be married."

"All right. I can do that for you. Let me go get a witness." He glanced down at Josie. "Think the dog should go outside?"

Abe chuckled. "Josie's going to be my stepdaughter, Father. She'd better stay for the wedding." Martha lipped a "Thank you" to him as they took their places.

The short ceremony ended almost before it began. "You may kiss the bride," the man intoned after he said the last prayer.

Sudden terror swept through Abe. Why hadn't he thought about that? Should he just grab her and kiss her as if it were natural? No, that would be breaking her trust. "I'm sorry, Father, I can't do that. My bride's very shy."

The man nodded.

Abe pulled out a generous donation and placed it in the man's hand, an act that brought a grateful smile. "Thank you, thank you," the man said. "May you live long and happy lives together."

"Do we need a marriage certificate?" Abe asked.

"Oh, yes, yes, you do." He pulled one from a small box in the corner, and they all signed it.

Then the priest wished them well and ushered them through the place where the door should have been.

"Now, back to the claims office," Abe said, walking down the street.

sixteen

Martha felt a big letdown as Abe led her to the claims office. But what had she expected? She'd made it plenty clear to him that he would be only a friend. If he so much as pecked her on the cheek, she'd probably take off into parts unknown. He knew that and she had to admit the truth of it. Why the disappointment then?

"Here we are," Abe said, sounding a little excited. "Are you ready to become a landowner?"

"Yes," she murmured. "Let's go in."

As they entered the office, Josie stayed at Martha's side. Half an hour later, they emerged with a piece of paper worth more than gold. "We did it," Abe said, looking as though he'd like to dance a jig.

She met his happy eyes. "Almost," she corrected. "Didn't he say we have to move up the creek a little farther?"

He nodded. "We don't care though, do we? That's better than getting kicked out when they survey the town . . .in a couple of weeks, didn't he say?"

"Yes." Suddenly, she needed to see if their new place was as nice as the one they'd picked out. "Let's go look at it."

"I was about to suggest the same thing." His brown eyes twinkled brightly. "You know what they say about married people. . .that they even think alike."

Martha gave him a small push. "That means after they've been married a hundred years. Come on, let's see if we like our claim."

They walked east until they passed the place where they'd sat earlier while she'd proposed to him. As she thought about that, her face grew hot way back to her ears. He'd probably never let her forget that she'd been the one to propose.

"He said the two trees leaning over the creek are the first trees on our land," Abe said as they hurried along. "There they are!" They walked on until he stopped dead. "We're on our own land, Martha!" he shouted. "This is our claim." Josie stopped short, looked to see if something was wrong, gave her plumy tail one wag, and splashed into the creek.

Martha looked down the creek and the several more trees beside it. Then she swung her gaze away from the creek. Beautiful, gently rolling land with several small knolls suitable for building. She glanced toward Abe to find him watching her.

"Is it all right?" he asked softly.

"It's perfect, Abe, even better than the other." She turned around to face the creek. "Look, you can't see the old Fort Walla Walla buildings from here. I like that a lot better." She whirled around to face the large area of land. "Come show me where we'll build. Am I going to help build our house?"

He laughed, looking pleased. "It'll be a big help. . .if you really want to. It'll go up a lot quicker. You tell me where you'd like it."

She shook her head. "Almost everywhere looks good to me."

When Abe's eyes kept straying to Martha's hand, she knew he wanted to take it but he didn't. "Come on," he said, "let's walk until we see a spot just screaming for a house." He laughed again and met her eyes. "I noticed you didn't call it a cabin."

It didn't take them long to agree on a small rise about 100 feet back from the creek. "We don't want to be too close to the creek," Abe said, "because someone else will get the property on the other side. We wouldn't want someone else in our front yard."

Martha agreed. "Let's scratch the house on the ground," she suggested after they'd walked and talked for more than an hour.

"We have to make some plans first. Draw it out on paper. Want to go do that now?"

She did, so they hurried back to town. When they reached the boardinghouse, he started to go in.

"Let's draw it out at the wagon," she said. "I feel strange in there."

"You won't after I tell her we're married."

"You can't do that, Abe! We have to keep it secret until we get the house built."

He looked puzzled. "Why do we have to do that?"

He knew. Why did he want to make her explain it?

"You know, Abe. People might think it's funny."

Recognition jerked into his eyes. "Oh, I understand. But you're my wife now, Martha, and I don't want you out there alone. It's dangerous. I didn't marry you to let some no-good cur come along and hurt you."

She felt her face growing hot again. "But they'd expect us to sleep in the same room, Abe. I don't think they even have a spare room."

He sighed. "All right, let's go to the wagon to draw out the plans. We'll figure this out later." They walked a few feet when he stopped. "Got any paper at the wagon?"

"Just that torn piece I've been keeping track of my bills

to you on."

He grinned. "I guess you can forget those bills now. Let's go get some paper. You been inside the store?"

She shook her head. "Only to ask for work. I haven't had any money." She felt excited to be going in at last. She'd been tempted to explore the place on several occasions when she'd been bored and lonely. But with so few people around they'd know she was the girl in the wagon with no money. She couldn't handle that.

Abe opened the door and stood back to let her in first. She stepped in. Several tables, built from long, half-logs and laying on blocks, stood on the dirt floor. Clothes, pots and pans, garden tools, and other exciting-looking things nearly hid the boards. Abe led the way to a half-log table holding tablets, separate sheets of paper, pencils, pens, both quills and fountain pens, and bottles of ink. It all looked fascinating to Martha. She'd like one of everything.

He chose a large writing pad with the words *Pencil Tablet* on the front. "You do have a pencil?" he asked.

"Yes," she whispered, then wondered why. "It's not very good, but it writes."

He picked up a pencil. "See anything else you need?" he asked.

See anything else she needed? Only everything. But she couldn't tell him that. "Do you need a ruler?" she asked. "You know, for the walls and things?"

He smiled and nodded. "Good thinking, wife."

Martha jerked her head around to see if anyone else had heard, but they were the only customers at the time. He picked up a twelve-inch ruler, and they carried the things to the man at the front of the store.

"Figgerin' to do some writin'?" the man asked with a

grin as he added the amounts. "That'll be forty-five cents," he said. "Need somethin' to put that in?"

"Nah," Abe said. "We got four hands." He handed the pencil and ruler to Martha, and they left the store.

"That store wasn't nearly as grand as the ones I used to shop in," she said, "but it was fun. I haven't been in a store for almost nine months."

"Well, it won't be that long before you go again." They reached the wagon, and Josie rushed under the wagon and closed her eyes. Abe sat on one dynamite box and shoved the other one to Martha. "You got something hard we can put under this here paper?"

Martha could think only of the big Bible, and it was too special to use for that. "I don't think so. Sorry." Then her eyes fell on the box she was about to sit on. "What if we turned the box over, put the tablet on it, and sat on the ground beside it?" A moment later they sat side by side with the tablet before them, the pencil in Abe's right hand.

"Draw," Martha urged. "I can't wait to see our new house."

Abe laughed into her eyes. "It isn't that simple. We have to decide how big it will be and what we need in it."

She extended her arms, her fingers bent forward. "Big. We want it big. It'll have a fireplace, won't it?"

He nodded. "It'll have to." He leaned over the paper a moment, making several dots along the edges. "Thirty feet by twelve looks good to me. What do you think?"

She shrugged. "I have no idea what thirty feet would look like."

For a moment, he checked distances on the ruler then drew a ten-inch line, then a right angle and four inches, then another ten-inch line and a four-inch connecting line at the beginning end. He grinned at his drawing. "That's purty good if I do say so myself. Now, we need a bedroom on each end, nine feet by twelve." He cut off three inches at each end, leaving a large four-inch—really twelve-foot—room in the middle. "This is the kitchen and main room. We'll put a fireplace in the middle so we can cook on it and it'll heat the whole house." He looked up. "What do you think, wife?"

"I love it. And it seems huge. Are you sure we can afford such a fine house?"

"I think we can. If it'll make you happy, I know we can. Well, I'd better ride up Mill Creek to the sawmill and order the lumber. I don't know how long it'll take them to get it made up." He got up from the ground and flexed his legs, limbering them up from sitting on the ground. "Hey, I'm hungry. Let's go have some supper at one of the saloons."

She twisted her head back and forth. "You know I don't go to saloons."

He reached for her arm. "Come on. I go to them all the time and never have alcoholic drinks. They serve meals, too, you know. There's nothing inside that would shock or hurt you, especially with me beside you." He watched her for a moment then laughed. "I suppose I can keep buying bread for you if that's what you'd rather eat. How about a brimming bowl of hot stew? Doesn't that sound better?"

It did sound good. "All right, I'll go. Just once to see how it is."

When they stepped into the saloon, Josie tried to slip in between their feet. "The dog can't come in," the barkeep called.

Abe took her collar and led her out. "I'll bring you something when I come out," he promised in a whisper.

Abe bought Martha a big bowl of hot vegetable stew and a sandwich with a cup of coffee. She stuffed herself again. Before they left, Abe bought another large roast meat sandwich that he held until they reached the wagon. Then he slipped it to Josie who eagerly accepted it and carried it under the wagon.

"Well, what are we doing about tonight?" he asked Martha.

"I don't understand," she said. "We'll do as we always do, won't we?"

"No, we won't do as we always do. I have a wife now, and I intend to protect her. Are you coming to Martin's Boardinghouse, or am I staying here?"

seventeen

Martha drew in a deep breath. What did he mean? He'd promised her they'd be friends. "I can't go to Martin's," she said in a quavering voice, "and you can't stay here." She took several more deep breaths and felt a little better. "You promised, Abe."

His eyes hardened, his mouth thinned into a straight narrow line, and the cords in his neck stood out. "I don't remember promising to let you take unnecessary chances." He met her eyes with defiance, then his shoulders slumped. "I'll sleep on the ground here." He looked around, hesitated a moment, then grinned. "In fact, if I freeze, that may hurry the house along."

Martha wanted to protest his sleeping on the ground, but where else was there? "I can let you have a couple of blankets," she whispered in a stricken voice.

"I have plenty of blankets," he said. "I didn't get paid half the time in the army, but I got a little bedding out of it."

He marched off, returning ten minutes later with a half-dozen dark wool blankets and a fat pillow. He arranged the bedding on the grass behind the wagon. "Now, Miss Prim," he said, "I doubt anyone will know I'm here. I know you don't want me to touch you, but would you consider praying together each evening?"

"Yes, I'd purely like that." So they prayed together for the first time, each thanking God for the other and asking Him to bless their marriage. Then each fell into their own bed to ponder the many happenings of the day.

Martha admitted to herself that she'd married a true gentleman who would never break a promise to her or anyone else. She thanked God again for Abe, then asked His protection on them both. She told Him that now she knew how much He loved her and thanked Him for leading her into this marriage where she'd be purely happy. She fell into a deep sleep, her arm around Josie.

❧

A beautiful baritone version of *Amazing Grace* awakened Martha in the morning. Josie didn't flick an ear. "You're getting used to my new husband already," she whispered to the relaxed dog.

"Hey, anyone in there?" he called after finishing the third verse.

Martha threw the covers back and reached for her clothes. She bathed every single day before dressing, but she felt embarrassed this chilly morning.

"Don't get up," he called. "I just wanted to tell you I'm going to Martin's to get cleaned up. I'll be back in a half-hour."

As she heard his footsteps fade away, Martha slumped back into her warm nest. Then she jumped out, grabbed her wash bowl, poured ice cold water into it, and proceeded to get herself as clean as possible. Pretty clean, too, she told herself through chattering teeth.

When Abe returned, Martha and Josie were playing tag around the wagon in the sunshine. "Let's go get some breakfast," he said. "We can get Josie's bones while we're out. Then I have to ride up Mill Creek to the sawmill."

Martha wanted to go in the worst way. Was it proper for wives to tell their husbands when they wanted something? She didn't know but she had to anyway. "If you'd let me ride Sampson again, I'd love to go with you," she asked, almost afraid to hear his answer.

A smile broke over his face. "I forgot to tell you Sampson is my wedding present to you."

Sampson! Abe was giving the horse to her? Martha wanted to throw her arms around his neck to show her appreciation. But he'd never understand.

"What a lovely gift! But I have nothing for you, Abe. What can I give you?"

He smiled and his arms twitched as if wanting to be somewhere they weren't. "You already have," he told her. "Marrying me was the best gift in the world. And I'd love to have you ride up Mill Creek with me. But what about Josie? She'd never make it, Martha. But right now let's go eat."

After eating stacks of pancakes and bacon smothered in maple syrup, they went to the meat shop for Josie's bones and hurried back to the wagon. "Did anyone know you didn't sleep in your room last night?" Martha asked, resting on a box while Josie chewed the bones noisily.

He sat on the other box and sighed. "I'm stuffed. How about you, wife? No, as far as I know, no one knows where I slept except you two girls." He chuckled. "If you don't tell, I won't." After a short silence and while Josie crunched bones, Abe looked at Martha again. "But someone will get suspicious when I do it every night. Why don't we go ahead and tell people we're married? No one's going to come out here in the middle of the night to check on newlyweds."

After thinking a bit, Martha nodded. "You're right. My mother always told me to tell the truth, and it's still best."

"All right!" Abe said with a relieved look. "Now, what did you decide about riding up Mill Creek with me?" He grinned. "You could ride your new horse."

Martha could hardly wait to see her new horse, let alone ride him. He'd surely seem different now that he was hers. All hers. "I want to go really bad," she said. "Do you think it would be all right to tie Josie up for so long?"

Abe nodded. "Those bones will last her a long time. If we get out of here quick we'll be back sooner." He put the rope he'd used before around the wagon tongue again and tied it to Josie's collar. "Let's get out of here," Abe said softly, giving Josie a few strokes.

Abe handed Martha some money with instructions to get some sandwiches while he saddled the horses. This time she didn't hesitate before going into the saloon, and she returned with four roast meat sandwiches. The barkeep didn't mention what kind the meat was and as far as Martha could tell no one ever asked. She didn't either.

A half-hour later, the two horses walked up the slowly climbing path beside Mill Creek. Martha noticed the creek had more water here than down by their place where it crossed the street. Soon they came to the sawmill and Martha thrilled as Abe ordered the lumber for their house. As she watched and listened to the transaction she noticed that other men respected and listened to Abe. What a truly good man. She felt proud of him and was overjoyed to be building a home with him. Maybe if she tried hard she could fall in love with him. But, rather than the glow of love, she felt unbelievable gratitude for what he'd done for her, the excitement of not being alone anymore, or destitute, and of having property, and lastly, of building a home.

On their way home again, she wondered why the horses couldn't have pulled a wagon with the lumber.

"That would be horribly hard for them, even if I didn't

haul much at a time," he explained. "I'd rather pay for the hauling and save the horses' good health. We'll be able to start building sooner, too. It would have taken dozens of trips with the saddle horses. They'll do it in about four with the big wagons and horses."

Martha again felt thankful for having such a kind man. And, as for the house, she knew they'd be in before too many weeks had passed. She could already see it in her mind.

When they reached the wagon, Josie greeted them eagerly, forgiving them for having left her.

‎ ⍦

The next day Martha decided to do her washing while Abe prepared the site for the house. Abe still had his things washed at the boardinghouse so she didn't have much to do. "When I finish, I'll come over and help," she called as he trudged off toward their place.

It didn't take her long to get her few things washed, rinsed, carried back to the wagon, and hung on the large weeds. When she hung the last garment, she saw the three Indians coming across the expanse of grass. *Abe*, she thought, *why aren't you here?* But she went forward to greet the tall men, a smile pasted tightly on her face. Their stench reached her before they did; she swallowed and became determined to be cordial.

They greeted her and walked toward her wagon. One of them held a bunch of wild onions in his hand. Another held something she couldn't make out, and the last had a large piece of meat. When they reached the wagon they held their offerings to her. "Food," one said, gesturing toward the cook pots.

"I don't have anything to make fire," she said but saw immediately they didn't understand. She made motions of starting a fire then shook her head. "No fire," she repeated one time after another.

"No fire," one finally repeated. Then he held up his wild onions. "Soup," he said plainly. Oh, she was supposed to make soup.

She shook her head, put the kettle on, and stuck her hand into the cold ashes. "No fire," she repeated. Then she searched over the ground a little and repeated, "No fire."

One of the Indians nodded. "No fire." He started off at a slow gait and the other two followed. She dropped to one of the dynamite boxes and heaved a big sigh. At least she was rid of them for one more day. Tomorrow could worry about itself. But before she collected her clothes and went to help Abe, they returned, stink and all.

One knelt before the fire pit arranging various pieces of wood he'd brought, another handed her two hands full of potatoes. "*Wapatoes*," he said, pointing to the potatoes. "Soup."

A small wisp of smoke told Martha she might as well get busy and make a big kettle of soup. She washed the meat, cut it up, and dumped it into the water, then added the potatoes and wild onions. That stuff would take a long time to cook so, though barely able to stand not knowing what was happening at the place, she might as well forget about helping Abe.

The Indians sat on the ground around Martha and watched the pot begin to steam. "Food," one said. "Cook," the second one added.

"Fire," Martha said giggling, pointing to the flames.

"Fire," they all repeated.

"Box," Martha said clearly, touching her seat.

They all smiled as they repeated the word.

She pulled off a few blades of grass and said the word, which they all repeated several times, each pulling pieces of grass. They wanted to learn English! So, all the while the soup cooked, she told them words while showing them what it was, and they repeated it. Every once in a while she'd say a word they'd just said and one of them would point at the object. They weren't dumb.

Martha became so involved in their word game she forgot all about going to the place. And the Indians forgot about eating. The fire maker kept the fire going as Martha worked with them.

Finally, she remembered the soup and discovered it was all cooked. She filled three mugs with the soup and offered it to them. One of them pointed to Martha, saying, "Soup." Why not? she thought.

She'd just filled a mug for herself when Abe hurried toward her from the street. "Are you all right?" he called, reaching her before she could answer.

"I'm fine," she said. "I just got invited to cook some soup. Want some?"

He did, so she gave him some, wondering if the Indians would be upset. But they weren't. Each ate another cupful, thanked her in English, and drifted across the prairie.

"I'm sorry I wasn't here for you," he said. "Were you frightened?"

"Not too much. I was mostly disappointed not to go see what you were doing. But you know what? They wanted to learn English. I taught them a bunch of words."

He laughed and patted her on the head. "Good little teacher," he said. "They'll be back."

Martha's blue eyes twinkled. "Maybe we can be in our new house first and they won't be able to find us."

"They'd find us if we moved to California," he said,

laughing. "They're part of the price we pay for living here." He ate another cup of soup. "Not too bad if a person doesn't like salt," he said. "I happen to like it very much. I'll get you some salt at the store before they come again."

❧

Three days later the wagons of lumber arrived. "We're ready to build a house," Abe said. "Think we can do it alone?"

Martha shrugged. What did she know about building a house? They worked the rest of the day trying to get the logs set up under the floor. When they quit they both cleaned up then bought supper and walked back to the wagon.

"Would you mind if I hired someone to help with the house?" he asked as they sat and dreamed about their new house.

She shook her head, surprised he'd bothered to ask. "Not if you think it's necessary. . .and we have enough money."

"If you'll come to my room at the boardinghouse some-time, we'll count our money together. Then we'll both know exactly how much we have left, and how careful we need to be." He got up. "I'll go find someone to work a couple of weeks." He lingered a moment as if he'd left something undone, but he made no move to touch her before striding down the path toward the street.

eighteen

Walking toward the saloon, Abe felt completely out of sorts. What kind of a marriage did he have, anyway? Well, he'd known how it would be. He walked into Galbraith's. "Anyone want a few weeks of hard work?" he asked loudly enough for everyone to hear, before settling onto a stool at the bar.

"What kinda work?" "Good pay?" "Who for?" all came at him immediately.

"For me, building my house," he announced to the room in general.

"What you wanna house for?" a tall blond-haired young man asked. "You ain't got no woman."

"Oh, he's sparkin' the little gal with the wagon," another answered.

Abe sipped the coffee the barkeep had set before him. "I took out a claim and now I'm building a house. Anyone want a few weeks' work let me hear."

The blond fellow moved to the stool beside Abe. "I might," he said. "I ain't got much goin' right now. If the price was right."

"I'll give you a fifty-dollar nugget if you help as long as I need you, somewheres around three weeks."

The man stuck out a white hand. "I'll be there in the morning at daybreak."

Abe paid the barkeep for two cups of coffee and hurried back to the wagon. While they relaxed on their boxes, he told Martha of the saloon talk. "It's a good thing we

136

decided to tell people we're married," he said. "I didn't say anything, but people'll find out I've been stayin' here."

She thought a moment and nodded. "You're right. You just go ahead and tell anyone you want. Will you still keep your room at Martin's?"

He nodded slowly. "Nowhere else to put things."

Abe soon decided to hitch the horses to the wagon and pull it to the place.

"It'll be nice to have all our things on our own place," Martha said, her cheeks flushed with excitement.

She looked so pretty and happy Abe wanted to snatch her and give her a kiss on the cheek. But his reply revealed none of his inner turmoil. "My things aren't here yet," he answered. "But it'll be nice to have the wagon and the horses there." He winked at her. "A little more privacy for the newlyweds, too."

❧

For the next two weeks, Abe worked hard, and so did Emil, his helper. Martha did any light work Abe assigned her and brought them tools, small items, and lunch from the stores and saloons so they could spend more time on the house. Her excitement grew as the house did.

One day as Martha and Josie brought hot roast meat sandwiches to the men, she realized her house looked like a real log house. The steep shake roof would keep out all rain and snow forever. Martha had been chinking the logs on the inside. She had more to do but not too much. Abe had built a rough, very rough, table and sideboard for the kitchen from half-logs. At least it would provide a place to eat and to store the few kitchen items Martha had in the wagon. The dynamite boxes would substitute for chairs for a while.

The main room had not one piece of furniture; the only

thing in the room was the stone fireplace in the center, for which she'd gathered rocks from Mill Creek. The big fireplace would easily heat the whole house. The kitchen and main room would each have two small windows to admit light; each of the bedrooms would have three windows. At the moment, although they had nothing inside, but they both had doors with locks, as did the main room. She'd braid some rugs to cover the rough floorboards.

"How long before it's finished?" she asked after giving them their lunch.

Abe wiped the sweat from his forehead. "Not too long. We still have to put the windows in. I've been holding out for glass windows but all I find in the stores are made of isinglass. Think you could handle them for a while?"

"You mentioned once that my. . .our. . .wagon doesn't even have doors. I can handle anything. I just want to move in. Could we do that without windows?"

He grinned, shoved in the last bite of sandwich, washed it down with coffee, and struggled to his feet. "I should say no," he said lightly, "but why would I? We're sleeping in the open, and I don't know about you but I'm waking up with a coating of frost every morning."

Martha looked as if he'd slapped her. "I'm sorry," she said softly. "I haven't been frosted, and I didn't even think about you being colder than I. You've never complained once." She giggled. "But you had a perfectly good bed at Martin's."

She'd never understand that, even if he froze to death, he wanted to be at least near her until she learned to love him—if she ever did. He picked up his hammer and went back to work.

That evening, after Emil left, they moved the things from the wagon into the house. Abe let Martha have her choice of the two identical bedrooms, and she chose the one on the east end of the house. They carried in all the clothes—hers, her mother's, father's, and Jackson's. Josie followed at their heels each time they carried a load from the wagon.

Then they put her few dishes, pans, and silverware on the sideboard shelves. Abe thoroughly enjoyed the work; he loved doing it together with Martha, and hoped she did, too. She put the dishrags and towels on shelves, then turned to him, laughing.

"We're all moved in, Abe. We just lack one thing. The food." She burst into merry laughter again.

Her happy sounds and looks clutched at Abe's stomach. How was he supposed to do this? But he joined her laughter. "Want to go get some things so we can start eating at home?"

She nodded gaily, then her face sobered. "What about wood for a fire? We can't cut down our precious trees, can we? We'll save them for shade along the creek, all right?"

She was very young and not at all pushy, but she sure knew how to press a point if it was important to her. He nodded. "Sure. I won't cut a single tree until you ask me to." Her sigh of relief was audible to him across the room.

It seemed she'd forgotten all about his things at Martin's, but he wanted them here in their home. Even with them, he still wouldn't feel married, but at least he'd feel he lived here. "Uh, I think I'll go clear out my room at Martin's."

"I'm sorry again, Abe. I'm thinking only of myself as you can see. I forgot all about your things. Let me go help you carry them."

"Sure. We can fill the saddlebags and let the horses

carry the stuff." They walked over, saddled the horses, put the saddlebags on, and led the horses to the boarding-house door. Then they carried everything from Abe's room and loaded it into the saddlebags. Abe brought out seven more army blankets and draped them over Charity's back behind the saddle. "Looks like we're ready to go," he said, swinging into the saddle.

Martha swung into her saddle, and they walked the horses the half-mile to their house where they unloaded the saddlebags and transferred the things into Abe's room at the west end of the building.

Later, Abe spread the seven blankets on the hard floor, feeling disgruntled and alone. He stormed into the living area and a moment later Martha came out, Josie so close behind that she almost walked on Martha's heels.

Abe pointed at the dog. "Don't you think the dog belongs outside?" he asked.

Martha's face turned white. "Why, Abe? What did she do?"

"Nothing, but dogs belong outside. Houses are for people."

She shook her still-pale face. "I don't feel that way, Abe. Josie belongs with me. Always."

Why should she get every single thing she wanted? And do nothing his way? Nothing at all! He started toward the front door. "Come on, Josie," he said gruffly as he opened it and pointed out. "Go on out. You can bark at the moon or something." Josie stood undecided, looking over her shoulder at Martha. "Go!" Abe said much louder. The dog gave Martha one more look and slunk through the door.

"Good night, Martha," Abe said in a crisp voice and turned back to his own room. He lifted his covers on his floor bed and crawled in. Before long he pushed some of the blankets off. This room kept out a lot of the cold even without windows.

When he felt settled down, he had his usual talk with God. "You think things are going all right?" he asked after he'd thanked Him for allowing them the nice house and, for the sixty-ninth time, the beautiful lot the house sat on. His usual peaceful feeling didn't come. "You saw what I did just now, didn't You?" he asked. "Not only was I mean to Martha, but I took my frustration out on an innocent animal. You know I don't want to be like that, God. I want to make her happy. The dog, too."

I understand, Abe. You'll do better tomorrow.

"But how is this arrangement fair to me?" he asked. "She's so sweet and beautiful that I ache for her, God. How long can I endure the pain?"

You're doing fine, Abe. I'm well-pleased with you.

"That's just great, but I ain't so pleased. You ever heard about unrequited love, God? It's something us mortals have to live through sometimes, and it hurts something awful. Livin' with her, I'll never be able to forget it. That's what made me act like I did tonight. And I didn't even mean what I said."

I saw, Abe. I was with you. It'll be easier if you can get it through your head that you're to be her friend and nothing more. Try hard to make your friend happy. Concentrate on making your place flourish, helping your town develop, and changing the wrongs into rights.

"You're the boss, God, but what I want is for my wife to love me as I love her." He received no answer and after turning over on the hard floor several times he fell asleep.

nineteen

Martha couldn't believe her ears. Abe couldn't be ordering Josie out of the house. Not Abe! She'd been terribly impressed with his kind attitude to animals as well as people. But she stood there and watched him order her dog from the house. Josie hadn't been separated from her since long before they left Missouri, and neither she nor Josie intended to ever be separated again.

She laid out her featherbed in shock. What happened? Hadn't she known Abe well enough? Was he going to be this way with the new house? She'd thought things were going perfectly, their new house nearly finished. Life looking good. Sometimes she hoped she'd feel a twinge of something special for Abe. But, oh, she felt something special for him all the time. Just as she would feel to her very best friend in the whole world. She loved him as a friend more than she could say. He'd been so good to her and Josie. She'd felt something. Something more than appreciation. But she'd hoped for something romantic.

She crawled into her warm nest, pulling the covers around her shoulders. "Dear Lord," she whispered into the dark room, "thank You for all the blessings You just keep pouring out on me. Help me to dwell on my blessings and forget my sorrows. Help me to be what You want me to be. . .especially to Abe. What happened tonight, ˈord? How should I handle—"

As she prayed, a small whine outside her unfinished window interrupted. "Should I bring her back in, Lord?"

She waited quietly for the Lord to show her but she felt nothing. Then another idea presented itself to her. "Or should I sleep with her in the wagon?"

Immediately she felt she should, that she could do that without defying Abe. She gathered up her featherbed and blankets and slipped out the front door where Josie met her, dancing with joy. She hurried out to the wagon.

Martha put her finger to her lips. "We can't make any noise," she told the jubilant dog who beat her into the wagon. In a few minutes they lay together as they had for these many months. Martha breathed a silent *Thank You, I love You* prayer and fell into a deep sleep.

ه

Martha pressed closer to Josie, realizing the cold even in her sleep. When she wakened in the morning she felt cold in spite of her blankets. She wished they could have a fire in the fireplace, but they had to let the mortar set for a week or so. Besides, they didn't have any wood.

Snuggling closer to Josie, she soon felt warm and cozy. She should get up and go into the house, but a few more minutes in her warm nest wouldn't hurt anything. "A little extra warmth never hurt anyone, did it?" she whispered into Josie's ear.

A few minutes later she heard the front door open and close firmly, then she noticed Abe walking toward the creek. When he reached the creek he looked east, then west, and returned to the house, circling it once before calling her name.

Then she realized he didn't know she'd come to the wagon, and probably felt uneasy. "We're all right, Abe," she called. "Over here, in the wagon."

He hurried over and looked at them. "I've been waiting for you to come out of your bedroom," he said.

"Finally I called. . .and you didn't answer."

Martha giggled. "Only because I didn't hear you," she said.

"I thought something had happened to you," he went on as though she hadn't spoken. He stood quietly looking at them for a long minute. "Why did you sleep out here?" he finally asked.

"Josie cried."

"Oh." He looked sadder than she'd ever seen him. Maybe he was sorry he'd been so harsh.

"If it means that much to you, Josie can live in the house."

She jumped from her warm bed before remembering she wore only a nightgown. Oh well, it covered her as well as a dress. She felt like hugging Abe for saying Josie could come inside. But she didn't. "Thank you," she said. "It does mean that much to me. I thought you felt the same way about her, Abe."

A strange look darkened his brown eyes. "You'd better go inside and get changed before you catch pneumonia," he answered in a froggy voice. Martha wondered if he'd caught a cold.

Martha wrapped the blankets around herself then dashed through the grass to the front door and into the house, Josie at her side. The house actually felt warm, even with no heat and the windows unfinished! She couldn't believe the difference! Keeping Josie with her, she went into her room and shut the door, only to discover she needed water. She snatched her little bucket and ran to the creek then came back and washed up in the icy water as she had been doing ever since she had run out of buffalo chips. When she finished, she dressed, then carried the water out.

"You really bathed in that creek water?" Abe asked.

She laughed. "I do it every morning. You've been using Martin's warm water. Are you brave enough to do it like I did?"

He looked almost sick. "I'm not sure I want to be clean that bad. Not until the sun warms us up a little, anyway. Are you ready to go get some breakfast?"

They'd talked about buying food yesterday but hadn't done it. "Why don't you get some food to cook here?" she asked. "Could we cook it outside? Or would you rather wait for the fireplace to cure?"

"Let's go eat first then buy some food. Know what else I have to do today?" he asked with an embarrassed grin.

She shook her head.

"Build an outhouse. We have just about enough logs left for that. And I guess nothing could be more important."

An outhouse! "Oh Abe, that will be wonderful! I will appreciate that more than you'll ever know."

So, before the sun dropped behind the horizon that night, a new outhouse stood about fifty feet southeast of the house. Martha put her second newest Montgomery Ward catalog inside.

Martha didn't feel as comfortable in the new house as she'd expected, and she kept Josie right with her all the time. She certainly didn't want her dog bothering Abe.

When bedtime came, Abe asked if they could read the Bible together before they prayed, and that delighted Martha. There was only one thing she wanted more than that. "Could we find out more about the Methodist church?" she asked after their prayers. "Where it meets and if they'd let us start going there?"

Abe laughed. "Churches are public places, Martha.

Anyone can attend. I'd really like to find a church to attend, too. It's been too long. I'll see what I can learn. Now, we better go to bed so we can get up in the morning. Good night."

Martha felt sorry for Abe when Josie followed her into her room and he went into his alone.

twenty

Abe jerked off his outer clothing and fell into his hard bed, thoroughly disgusted with himself. Why had he been so cruel to Martha and Josie? He knew the answer to that question almost before he asked it, and it certainly wasn't their fault. He'd been frustrated by finally realizing that their marriage truly was in name only.

But that was no excuse! He'd been the one to push this sham of a marriage, and now he'd have to learn to live with it. He angrily turned over to discover he didn't feel any more comfortable on his left side. "I'm sorry, God," he whispered. "Will You forgive me? I'm a poor excuse for a man."

You're my child, and I love you. Don't be discouraged. I'm going to bless you in ways you can't even imagine. And I'll forgive you for being unkind, but only after you ask the same question of Martha. You hurt and confused her, Abe.

Abe jumped up from his uncomfortable blankets. He didn't want God's nebulous blessings. He wanted Martha to love him as he loved her! Then he remembered he'd also been told he hurt and confused her. He nodded. He'd done that all right. How could he make it up to her?

First off, he'd better let her know Josie had nothing to do with it. As he paced in his room, deep in thought, he noticed once again how barren it looked. Realizing Martha's looked the same, he wondered if he could make her some furniture. He laughed aloud at the thought. He'd never seen such a mess as the table and sideboard he'd

147

built. Well, he'd make her a bed and armoire, and he'd do a good job. Maybe he could make some plans before he started, sort of figure it out like he did the house. The house had turned out all right, even if he did say so himself.

He pulled on his clothes, lit a candle, opened his bedroom door, and slipped into the living area. He'd just find that paper and see if he could come up with something better. But he couldn't see well enough by the candlelight. Knowing he couldn't fall asleep yet, he quietly opened the outside door and stepped into the much colder night air.

Hunching against the cold, he headed toward the street, thinking how Martha must have suffered last night as well as all the other recent nights in the wagon. Both saloons were still brightly lit and loud voices could be heard as Abe walked past. Although tempted to go inside for the company, he walked to the end of the street, turned south until he passed the buildings, then turned east and walked briskly back to his house. He smiled. It wasn't a cabin but a house. Martha said so. Thinking of Martha and how much he loved her helped Abe feel better. Somehow he'd reach into her heart, he thought as he undressed for the second time that night. He crawled into bed telling himself that being unkind to her and Josie wouldn't win her love very fast. He'd do better in the future. Feeling more relaxed and less angry with himself, he dropped off to sleep.

❧

"I can't wait to be able to cook here," Martha said the next morning. "That's when it will seem like home. Think the fireplace will be cured in another week?"

He thought so and wondered how he'd get firewood, but didn't mention it to her. "I was just thinking," he said, "that I should get some good lumber and try making you a bed and armoire. Don't laugh."

Martha's blue eyes twinkled merrily. "I'm not laughing, Abe. I think that would be purely nice. I could put my featherbed on it and be as cozy as I was back home."

Abe felt gratified that she'd acted as though she'd forgotten his little fit. But he still had to apologize and ask her to forgive him. Of course, she would. She'd never hold a grudge. But, as the day progressed, he didn't apologize and things still seemed all right. About midmorning he took Charity and rode out to the Mill Creek lumber mill to order lumber and to check around for wood supplies. On the way he found plenty of downed trees, but he realized he'd need a saw and a way to haul the wood down to the place.

After ordering the lumber, he headed Charity back home. When they reached the village, he decided to check into a bar just to see what had been going on.

"Been missin' you," the barkeep said, pouring Abe a cup of coffee. "Ya heard the town's got a new name?"

"No. You mean newer'n Waiilapptu?"

"Yep, it's Walla Walla and, from what I hear, that's what it's gonna stay."

Abe took a long swig of the strong brew, swallowed, and exhaled the hot steam. He nodded. "Walla Walla. Where many waters meet. Good. It shoulda been Walla Walla all the time."

The barkeep had something else trying to pop out of him so Abe patiently waited.

"Now they're thinkin' on namin' the state Walla Walla," he said eagerly. "Wouldn't that be somethin'?"

"Yeah, that sure would be something. Think there's much chance?"

The barkeep scrubbed the shiny wooden bar top. "Some

think so. Guess we'll know sometime next year."

"You know what else they're doin'?" the barkeep asked almost immediately. "They're layin' out the town right away. Ain't that a scream? What's to lay out? One street. One dinky street built on an Indian trail. You and I could do that, Abe. Save hirin' the hi' falutin' surveyor they got comin' in."

Abe couldn't wait to relay the news to Martha.

"I'm purely thrilled with our town's new name," she said. "Walla Walla. Many waters. That's so nice the Indians will even be happy about it."

❧

Together they checked the street every day for the surveyor. Sure enough one day they found a man with his three-legged instrument in the middle of the street, peering first in one direction, then another. After keeping at it for more than a week, word got around that four of the eight buildings on the main street—the trading post, the tin shop, the vacant store, and Galbraith's Saloon—stood in the way of the proposed cross streets and would have to be either razed or moved.

What an uproar that caused!

"They can just get someone else to survey the town," Galbraith said one day while Abe and Martha ate dinner in his saloon. "They ain't tearin' my place down fer some street that ain't even there yet."

Abe worked most of every day on Martha's bed but, in the evenings, he always put his ear to the ground. Finally, when a full-fledged revolution seemed ready to erupt, he called the men of the town together.

"Do we or don't we want our town to grow?" Abe asked. "We'll all be better off financially, and we'll be more comfortable, too, when it's a little bigger. Why don't we all get together and move the buildings off the streets? It won't take long if we all help."

"Ain't a one of them buildings won't fall apart if we try to move 'em," Rackett, the owner of the tin shop said.

"Yeah," Galbraith added, "and I've already built the inside of mine. Cain't move that."

"Sure we can," Abe said. "What we can't move, we'll tear down and rebuild." He laughed softly. "We're only talkin' about four buildings. I built my house in a couple of weeks, and there's a lot more to it than any of these here stores. If we all help, we can do each one in less than a week, and they'll be better'n they were before. But we better get on it before it gets any colder."

Finally, with no real choice, the men agreed, and they set the next day to start on Reece's vacant store on the bank of Mill Creek.

It, as well as most of the other buildings didn't have a floor to support the walls in a move so they ended up tearing it apart and rebuilding it on the spot the surveyor had designated. It took three days and ended up sturdier than before. The next day they started on the tin shop.

As Sunday neared, Martha asked Abe if he'd learned anything about where the Methodists were meeting.

Abe laughed. "Sure did, but I doubt there'll be a meetin' this week. It's been meeting in Galbraith's Saloon, but he's gettin' ready to move. He was the most upset of any of the fellows, so I'm guessin' he's not about to be bothered with anything this week. Maybe we'll have him all moved and happy by next Sunday."

So Abe and Martha had their private Bible study together as they had been doing since they'd been married.

❧

Early the next morning Abe decided it was time to get some wood and get the fireplace going. "Think we could take the top off the wagon and whatever else we could to lighten it?" he asked Martha.

She thought a moment. "I guess we could, but why?"

"So I can haul some wood down from the mountains. It's going to be hard for the horses, and any weight I can dump will save them."

Her sudden smile brightened her entire face, almost the whole room. "Yes, Abe, take everything off but the wheels if you want, just get that wood."

Together they removed every bit possible without disabling the wagon. After Martha went inside to do something, Abe checked the wagon once more for anything removable. When his eyes hit the wagon floor again, he noticed the double floor. If he could get that first layer of boards off it would lighten the wagon a lot. Using his pry bar, he finally got the first board off. Then the second. When he lifted the third board he noticed a small pouch between the third and fourth boards. Curious, he pulled off the rest of the boards, picked up the pouch, and hurried inside the house. "See what I found between the two floors of the wagon?"

Martha peered at the pouch. "That's Papa's money pouch," she said. "I wonder how it got in there?"

Abe grinned. "It got in there when he put it there and nailed the second floor on. He hid it there, Martha. Open it up."

She opened it and pulled out money. Lots of money. They counted it out on the table. "Twelve hundred dollars?" Martha asked incredulously. "And you've been feeding me!"

"I like feeding you," Abe said. "Didn't you say your folks sold a farm just before you started west?" She nodded. "Well, that's the money. It was supposed to get your family started here." Suddenly, he hoped she wouldn't decide she didn't need him anymore.

Martha nodded, looking sad. "The money's yours," she told Abe. You've been paying for everything for-ever."

Abe shook his head. "It isn't mine. It isn't all yours, either. Some of it would be for your two brothers. But you'll still have enough left to care for yourself a long, long time. . .if you decide you don't need me anymore."

Her blue eyes opened wide. "Are you trying to get rid of me?"

"No. That's the last thing I'll ever want."

She relaxed. And smiled. "Good. I'm here to stay then. Now, may I go with you after wood?"

"I'd like that more than you know," he said, "but you'd better stay here. I may walk all the way back if I get too much wood. I'll just have to see how it goes. Anyway, I'll be back by dark."

❧

A little while later, after stopping at the general store for a large saw, he took off. He didn't hurry the horses but they reached the timber in a couple of hours. The spicy smell of the woods together with his new saw made him eager to start cutting logs. He soon found a large pine tree that had blown down. That single tree would fill the wagon to capacity. After four hours of backbreaking labor, he had the wagon stacked with wood—and he hadn't used the entire tree. If he ever got rested up from this, he'd come back and get the rest of the tree. And more.

The horses struggled with the loaded wagon but managed to drag it home.

Darkness had cloaked the town for less than an hour when he finally reached home. The horses nickered joyfully, as happy to be finished with their labor as Abe.

He unharnessed them and rubbed them down, took them

to the creek to drink, then fed them their oats and staked them out in the grass.

He knocked on the door in order not to startle Martha, but when he went in he found Nellie Martin there.

"You look tired and dirty," Martha said, laughing.

"I am tired and dirty," Abe agreed. "So are the horses."

Nellie edged toward the door. "I'll go now, Martha. You come over and see me, hear?" She turned to Abe. "You sure have built a nice place here, Mr. Noble."

"Thanks," Abe said with a pleasant smile. "We're enjoying it." He poured a basin of water and washed his face and arms while Nellie left. "Ready to go eat?" he asked as soon as the door closed behind the girl. "I'm starved."

An hour later they both carried a big load of groceries. Martha put the things on the table, then into the sideboard. Potatoes, cabbage, carrots, onions, salt pork, bacon, coffee, sugar, salt, beans, dried apples, flour, lard, dried corn, and cornmeal. They'd also found a little honey, for which they'd paid dearly.

"I never saw so much food in my life," Martha said. "I doubt we'll ever have to buy food again."

Abe grinned. "You'll be surprised how fast that goes." He winked at her. "I'm counting on you making some good meals now."

❧

The next morning Abe worked on Martha's bed before going to the village to help move the buildings. After a while he came home and finished the bed. Martha laid her featherbed on top of it and the blankets over that.

"Thank you," she said sincerely. "It's nicer than I hoped."

He felt his face grow warm under her compliments. "If you like it well enough, I'll make you an armoire next."

"I do. I'll love the armoire, Abe."

He then left to go downtown to move more buildings.

By the following Sunday, two more buildings stood in their new homes, leaving only Galbraith's Saloon left to move. Galbraith had put his off until last, maybe hoping it wouldn't really happen.

"If we knew who the Methodists are, we could invite them here for a week or two," Martha said.

Abe shook his head. "They'll be meetin' soon enough. Then we can go and see how things are."

After their own little Sunday school, Martha and Abe went riding, with the much stronger and fatter Josie running along beside them. When they returned, Abe rubbed the horses down while Martha prepared their supper. "You two are looking good," he said to Charity. "You're both shiny and fat. How do you like our new home?" He took them down to the creek, then out to a new spot of grass and staked them. He walked out a little farther, wondering if he should make a barn before winter. Everyone said it was so mild here that animals didn't need protection, but he wasn't sure. Charity had always had protection. Finally, he told the horses good night and went into the house.

Something smelled so good it made his mouth water. "All right, what is it?" he asked Martha.

Tendrils of her dark hair curled around her face that had turned pink from the fire. And her bright blue eyes sparkled with joy. "I made a dried apple pie," she said, pushing a curl behind her ear. "Come on, Abe, it's all ready."

The sight of his beautiful wife who wasn't his wife thwarted his appetite and made his heart beat so loudly he thought she'd hear it.

twenty-one

"Come on, Abe, let's eat," Martha said, but Abe didn't move. Standing there, looking at her, an expression of pain crossed his face. What could he be thinking? "Abe, are you all right?"

He jumped as if startled and moved to the table where he sat on one of the dynamite boxes from the wagon. After asking God to bless their food and them, he began reaching for food and serving her, then himself. "How did you make a pie?" he asked. "I thought you had to have an oven."

She laughed. "Papa brought a dutch oven from Missouri. You can bake over a fire in one, but it doesn't work nearly as easy or as well as an oven. Maybe I made a mistake baking the pie." She laughed again. "I wasn't going to mention it yet, Abe, but I purely want a stove. Mrs. Martin has one so I know they can be had. Do you think we could get one someday?"

At last Abe laughed, and laid down his fork. "I'm sure we will someday, Martha, but I'm not sure when. I don't know how to get one or how much it might cost." He sat quietly for a few seconds then retrieved his fork and continued eating the roast they'd gotten at Shaffer's last night. Finally, his eyes met hers. "I have something to show you after we finish. Do you have time?"

What could he have to show her that would take time? "I have the rest of my life," she finally said, trying to read his eyes. His appreciative smile looked so beautiful she almost had to catch her breath.

"It won't take that long," he said in breathy softness. "In fact, it won't take long at all. Maybe a half-hour."

They finished eating in almost silence as Martha tried to figure out what he was going to show her. He'd been outside for quite a while taking care of the horses. He must have seen something out there. Maybe a late-blooming wildflower. She noticed his empty plate. "Ready to try the pie?" she asked. Then she pulled the pie from the end of the table, cut it, and served the first piece to Abe.

"Heavenly," he breathed after the first bite. "When have we eaten anything to compare with this at the saloons?"

Martha shrugged and smiled. It tasted good to her, too, but she couldn't say that.

Abe's eyes twinkled. "If you can make things like this without a stove, I guess you don't really need one." He pushed his box back from the table. "I'm eager to show you what I mentioned," he said. "If you have the time, could we do it now?"

"I have the time, Abe. I'll get my coat."

"No, it's in my room. Shall I bring it out here on the table?" A minute or two later he returned and carefully emptied his pouch of gold on the opposite end of the table from where they'd eaten.

Martha had never seen so much money in her life. "Oh, Abe!" she cried, "we're rich."

"Get your dynamite box," he said, dropping to his own, chuckling. "We're far from rich, Martha, but let's see how much we have left." He separated the one-hundred-dollar nuggets from the smaller fifty-dollar pieces and counted them. "We have twenty of the big ones," he said, looking into Martha's eyes. "How much money is that?"

She thought a moment. "That's two thousand dollars."

He nodded. "Right. I knew I had a smart wife. Now, let's see, we have fifteen of the smaller nuggets. What's that?"

"You're testing me, Abram Noble. Well, it's about . . .seven hundred fifty dollars."

They counted out the paper money and what he had in his small pouch. "All right, tell me how much we have altogether."

"Looks to be about three thousand three hundred dollars." Her shining eyes met Abe's. "We are rich, Abe. We are."

He shook his light brown head. "Let me put it this way. Before we were married it was about four thousand three hundred dollars. We've used one thousand dollars, Martha. That's a fourth of it. We used most of it for lumber to build the house and furniture. Let's get our paper and decide what we'll do with the rest of it." He moved to his bedroom and brought back the tablet he'd bought the day they married.

He handed her the paper and pencil. "As we decide, you write it down. Now, first, do you have any idea how much a stove costs?"

She shook her head. "No, but I'll bet you do."

"I don't. So let's go to the next item. I'd like to buy some cows. Maybe about ten."

Her eyes widened. That sounded wonderful to her. She wanted nothing more than to have their own farm. She poised the pencil over the paper. "I love it, Abe. How much?"

"Something less than fifty dollars each, but let's say fifty dollars. How much, my little secretary?"

"Five hundred dollars. Oh, Abe, it does go fast doesn't

it? We really aren't all that rich. But could we have just a few chickens?"

He smiled and his eyes darted to her hand lying on the table. Martha tucked it down beside her. For a moment he looked cross but quickly recovered and continued. "People have cows for sale," he answered, "but I haven't seen any chickens. As soon as some arrive we'll be able to buy some chicks and raise them ourselves. We'll probably find some in the spring." His eyes sought hers again, but she noticed he kept them away from her hands. "Is there anything else you want?"

"Not that I can think of, but even buying groceries will eat up our money, won't it?"

"Not very fast. I promise you, we'll be able to eat and so will Josie and the horses. I'll also check at the store about a stove. See what they can do."

"I'd like a garden in the spring. That would help, wouldn't it?" she asked.

"Yes, we'll have a garden. We'll also send for some fruit trees early in the year." He pointed at the paper. "I don't know how much they'll cost, but write them down, anyway."

Martha felt thrilled from her nose to her toes. "Isn't it exciting, Abe? I love for us to talk like this. You know, about fixing up our place just like we want it. We're going to have a bit of heaven right here in Walla Walla County, aren't we?"

Once again an unhappy look crossed his face. She thought he was going to get up and leave, but he didn't. A forced smile appeared. "Yes," he said. "That's what we're going to have. A little bit of heaven right here." Then he did get up. "Want to take a walk along the creek?" He whistled for Josie, who struggled to her feet from her rug beside the fireplace, and the three took a long walk east along the creek.

❧

The next morning Abe worked on Martha's armoire for a little while then went downtown to help move Galbraith's Saloon, the last building to be moved. "It'll be the toughest, too," Abe said before leaving. "Galbraith will be watching everything we do to make sure we don't scratch a single board."

After he left, Martha cleaned up her little house, a job she considered pure bliss. Then she carried water, heated it, and washed their clothes, hanging them on big weeds when she'd finished. Josie followed her from weed to weed. "Washing our clothes sure isn't like those filthy things I washed at the creek, is it?" she asked Josie as they ran back to the house.

Inside, she started some bread. It would take all day to rise twice and bake in her dutch oven, but she had enough from the last batch for dinner. Abe always came home at noon to eat.

She sat down to mend another of her dresses, all of which seemed to be falling apart. One of these days she'd be repairing repairs. As she threaded the needle wishing she had a rocking chair to sit in while she worked, Josie started barking wildly, then the three Indians opened the door and walked in.

And so did the sickening smell! She jumped up and opened the front door and also the back door as wide as they'd go. Better to have the cool air than such a horrible smell—not that opening the doors would fix it.

They seemed to be wearing the same clothes as last time, the older one in buckskins and moccasins and the other two in white man's clothing, ragged and dirty. The older one looked into her eyes. "Food," he said.

Oh well, she'd better fix them something and get rid of them quickly so the place could be aired out before Abe came. She forced a smile to her lips and nodded. "Food," she repeated. She pulled out the last loaf of bread, cut it into thick slices, smeared lots of butter over them, then sliced the leftover roast from last night and put it over half the slices. Putting the sandwiches together, she laid each on a plate and handed it to the Indians who accepted the treat with happy smiles.

Just as one of the youngest started to take a bite, she told them to wait. "We have to thank the Great Spirit for giving us the food," she said, then proceeded to bow her head, close her eyes, and ask God to bless the food, the Indians, and her. When she opened her eyes, all three were gazing at her in awe. "Go ahead and eat," she said with a smile, making motions as though shoving a sandwich into her mouth.

The Indians looked at their sandwiches, and the older one lifted the top slice and started to put it to his mouth.

"No," Martha told him, "eat it all together." She put the top slice of bread back on and held the whole thing to his mouth. "Open wide, like this," she said, opening her mouth as wide as she could. When the Indian opened his mouth, she shoved the sandwich in and told him to bite off a piece—and he did!

That was all it took. They all sat on the floor and ate the sandwiches as she'd showed them. As they ate, one of the younger ones tapped the floor and looked at Martha with a question in his eyes. She tapped it as he had and said, "floor." They all repeated the word, tapping the floor.

They wanted to learn more words! Martha moved to the table, touched it, and said the word, after which they all repeated it. She went around the room pointing at things—fireplace, fire, window, sideboard, her own dress and shoes. The Indians became so engrossed in learning the words they nearly forgot to eat. She went through the list several times, then pointed to the objects while they said the words. They did much better than she'd expected. Finally, she told them to eat, simulating eating a sandwich, and they began eating again. When they finished their sandwiches they got up. Martha told them to say, "Thank you," which they did.

"Goodbye," Martha said as they left. They all smiled and repeated it, followed by something she didn't understand. Next time they came she'd start learning their language.

Abe didn't feel as excited about the visit as Martha did. "I need to be here all the time to protect you," he growled.

"No, you don't. Those men wouldn't hurt me. They're learning our language, and I'm going to learn theirs. Besides, Josie's always here."

Abe gave her a grudging smile. "You know what? We've never put that dog to the test. We don't know if she'd really protect you."

"Want to try beating me up?"

He stepped to the still-open door. "Nope. Gotta go though." He hurried off toward the village.

&

That evening Abe wanted Martha to go see how the town was getting laid out. They rode the horses as they did most evenings and wandered onto the street where small yellow flags had been attached to bars drilled into the ground at all four corners of each planned intersection. She saw many yellow flags but nothing north of the street except the Indian tepees.

"Those flags show the streets and their names," Abe said, pointing. "The north and south streets start at the creek with First Street. He's surveyed up to Fourth out about to where your wagon was."

"What about the east-west streets?" Martha asked. "Do they have names or are they numbered, too."

Charity moved around as though she'd like to get going; Sampson stayed as near to Charity as he could. "They have names," Abe said. "I understand they haven't decided whether the street will be Main Street or Nez Percé Street. The next one south is Alder, then Poplar, then Birch."

Martha laughed. "I like the tree names. But why are the markers so far apart?"

"The east-west streets are one hundred feet wide and the north-south streets are eighty feet." He laughed. "That's wider than the streets in Iowa where I came from. They think Walla Walla will be a huge metropolis."

Martha touched Sampson's sides with her heels. "Let's have a good ride tonight." Sampson took off without checking on Charity for once. After they'd ridden for a while they slowed. "I didn't see anything north of the street," she said.

He shook his head. "I think they decided not to bother the Indians. Although they have no legal claim to the land they might feel put out."

Later, when Abe came in from caring for the horses, he sat down on his box across the table from where Martha mended by candlelight. "I just remembered the lots on the street are for sale. Five dollars each, sixty feet wide and one hundred twenty feet deep. Should we buy some? They said we could buy two." She looked puzzled so he grinned and shrugged. "Who knows? Maybe we'll open a business someday."

She stabbed her needle through the fabric several times and laid it down. "Sounds good. I might even be able to help."

"Good. I'll do it tomorrow after we finish Galbraith's Saloon. Did I tell you it'll be finished tomorrow? Better than before, including the bar and stuff inside. Even Galbraith's pleased."

They had their Bible reading and prayer together and each fell into their own beds at opposite ends of the house.

&

Abe came home the next day wearing a wide smile. "I got the lots," he said. "I bought the second and third one, other than the businesses already established. Want to go see them?"

Martha laid down her dress that seemed to be more rips and tears than dress, and reached for her coat, Papa's coat, really. After a brisk walk, she learned their lots were #2 and #3 on the south side of the street between Reece's unoccupied building and the meat market. And a stone's throw from the creek.

"Oh, Abe, this is wonderful," she said. "We can start two businesses, each on our own lot."

He looked at her as if in shock. "So you want to keep our business lives as separated as our personal lives," he said. "Do you really dislike me that much?"

twenty-two

Abe wished right off that he hadn't said anything. He knew, almost knew, that Martha hadn't meant anything by her remark.

Her face blanched as she faced him. "I'm sorry," she said, the words rushing out together. She turned her back to him for a few seconds, then asked in a muffled voice if he was ready to go home.

They read their Bibles and prayed together before she broke down and cried. "I'm trying to be a good wife," she said when he pressed her to explain her tears.

"You're not trying to be a wife at all," he corrected, "but that was the agreement so I can't complain. You're being a good maid and cook, though. I couldn't ask for better."

Her blue eyes, bright with tears, met his. "Am I being a good friend?" she choked out.

He nodded. "Yes. You're definitely my best friend. Thank you for reminding me of that, Martha. I do appreciate you."

They fell into a routine with Abe working on her armoire most of the day while she did her housework, after which they spent at least an hour riding and exercising the horses. Then he went downtown to catch up on the news while she made supper.

One day he decided to look around in the general store and he found two things: a tool called a plane that McClinchey told him would smooth boards, and an envelope of plans to build furniture—tables, chairs, benches, beds, armoires, chiffoniers, and even cradles.

Excited, he bought both and couldn't wait to show the plans to Martha, which he did as soon as he walked through the front door. Unfolding it, he laid them on the table. After they'd enjoyed looking at the plans for several pieces of furniture, he pointed at the cradle. "See, there's even a plan for a cradle. Isn't it cute?"

Her face brightened until it looked almost sunburned. "I guess we won't need that."

He hadn't expected her to ask him to make a cradle right away but her words felt like icicles piercing his heart. He swallowed hard. "Never?" he whispered.

The cords in her throat tightened, and she didn't answer for a moment. "Never's a long time," she finally whispered back. After a moment she squared her shoulders. "I'm so glad you got that piece of paper, Abe," she said gaily. "By the time this winter passes we'll have the best furniture in town."

☙

When Sunday came, Martha and Abe put on their best clothes, she a dark blue muslin dress that hadn't been mended much, he a pair of dark cord pants and a light shirt. He didn't have a tie. She had to wear Papa's old coat over her dress as they walked to Galbraith's Saloon for church. The place had been cleaned up and four eight-foot long half-log benches had been put in against the east wall. A tall table in front would serve as a pulpit. After they found their seats, Abe happened to glance at Martha's face. He saw a disappointment he didn't understand, but a moment later it came to him. The only people there besides themselves were seven roughly dressed men and two Indians who made their presence known by their smell.

The service was simple. A pump organ had been brought in and placed against a wall, but no one played it as they sang several old hymns with gusto. Then Abe remembered that Martha played the piano. "Can you play that thing?" he whispered to her, gesturing toward the organ with his face.

She smiled and shrugged. "I don't know," she whispered back, "I've never tried."

The minister preached an impressive sermon about the shepherd leaving the ninety-nine sheep and searching for the one that was lost. "So you see," he finished, "we may think we're a long way from God way out here in the West, but He's right here with us. And He'd be much obliged if we'd do our part to help find his lost sheep. There are plenty out here."

After the service the men eagerly greeted Abe and Martha, telling them how much difference they made in the singing. Then the minister, Reverend Miller, welcomed them and asked them to be sure to return the following week.

"I'm sure we will," Abe said. "And I might be able to help you find someone to play that organ over there. My wife plays a piano. Maybe you'd let her give it a try?"

Reverend Miller wasted no time showing Martha to the instrument and how it worked. "Just pedal it a moment to get the feel," he suggested.

After a few pedals Martha tried the keyboard, which worked just fine, though sounding tinny.

"Say!" Abe said proudly, "that sounds as if you've been playing it forever."

Reverend Miller agreed. "It would be a great help if you'd play for us, Mrs. Noble."

Mrs. Noble! No one had ever called her that. Abe was a husband to be proud of. Besides being so good to her, he'd saved the town a lot of trouble when he'd gotten the men to rebuild the business buildings, and she'd heard them thank him several times. She agreed to play, and they went home to dinner and, later, a ride up into the mountains.

~

The days drifted past one after another as Abe built furniture, each piece looking better than the last, hauling wood from the mountains, and building a log barn and corral from small logs he brought down in the wagon.

Martha cleaned the house, washed and mended their clothes, and prepared good food for them. She played the organ each Sunday. Abe soon realized that her playing made them both enjoy the service more, giving them the feeling that they were a necessary part of the group.

Together, with Charity and Sampson, they'd driven home the ten, worn-out, skinny cows they'd bought from a man who'd just driven them up from Mexico. Abe, using wire from the store, had fenced in about twenty acres to make sure the cows got plenty of water and feed before the winter storms came.

Martha had been beside him helping him at every possibility. Her sweet disposition and helpful ways increased his love for her. Sometimes, the feeling of a one-way love caused him to be less than sweet to her, but her prompt and complete forgiveness only made him love her more.

The first snow flurries came early in December. At first it didn't stick, but then it came down in earnest and was a foot deep on the ground, the temperature hovering in the teens. Abe went out several times a day to feed the cattle and horses and to make sure the creek hadn't frozen, which it never did.

"Brrrr, it's plenty cold out there," he said one morning, setting the bucket of fresh milk on the floor beside the table. He held out his arms to the crackling fire. "Feels good in here."

She stood beside him. "You built us a fine house," she said. "I don't like to seem a snob, Abe, but we have by far the nicest home in Walla Walla. It's even warm and snug in this cold weather."

He couldn't hold back a wide smile. "You can say that anytime you want to. Don't you know it makes me feel good?"

Her bright blue eyes softened. "I thought it might." She quieted and looked thoughtful for a moment. "I really appreciate you," she went on. "Sometimes I wonder what would have happened to me if you hadn't come along."

A picture appeared in Abe's mind of his little Martha, sitting in the snow beside her wagon, snow sagging the canopy almost to the box. She wore her father's old coat as she tried to light a fire that only spit and smoked. "Let's just thank the good Lord we're together in this nice warm house," he finally said in a soft voice.

That night, after Abe went to bed, he thought about their lives. They'd been married nearly three months, and he loved Martha even more now than he had before. Martha couldn't be sweeter. Neither could she be a better help to him. But he wanted to touch her. Just pat her cheek, or hold her hand.

"What about it, God?" he asked. "Is this all there is?"

Isn't it enough, Abe?

"I don't know. What do You think?"

I think you have a lot more than most of the men in

the area.

Abe nodded his head in the dark. He sure did have more than most. He grinned in the dark. "You're right, Lord. I have plenty of food and the best woman in the world to prepare it for me. I have a warm place to live and the best woman in the world to keep it nice for me. Thanks, Lord, I should be more than satisfied. . .and I am. I'm plenty grateful for what You've given me. Maybe my marriage is a little different, but it's good. Thanks again, God. From now on I'll try hard to be satisfied with my lot in life. Help me, Lord. Help me be really satisfied."

You've learned a lot, Abe. I'm pleased with you. You're learning to be satisfied with what you have. But don't get too satisfied. Remember, Abe, I made you, I love you, and I plan the very best for you.

"Thanks, Lord. . . ." Abe rolled over, completely trusting, and fell asleep before he could tell God what he was thanking Him for.

A Letter To Our Readers

Dear Reader:

In order that we might better contribute to your reading enjoyment, we would appreciate your taking a few minutes to respond to the following questions. When completed, please return to the following:

Rebecca Germany, Editor
Heartsong Presents
P.O. Box 719
Uhrichsville, Ohio 44683

1. Did you enjoy reading *Martha My Own*?
   ☐ Very much. I would like to see more books
      by this author!
   ☐ Moderately
      I would have enjoyed it more if _____

   _____

2. Are you a member of *Heartsong Presents*? Yes   No
   If no, where did you purchase this book? _____

   _____

3. What influenced your decision to purchase
   this book? (Circle those that apply.)

Cover	Back cover copy
Title	Friends
Publicity	Other _____

4. On a scale from 1 (poor) to 10 (superior), please rate the following elements.

___Heroine   ___Plot

___Hero   ___Inspirational theme

___Setting   ___Secondary characters

5. What settings would you like to see covered in *Heartsong Presents* books?

_____

_____

6. What are some inspirational themes you would like to see treated in future books?_____

_____

_____

7. Would you be interested in reading other *Heartsong Presents* titles?   Yes   No

8. Please circle your age range:
   Under 18   18-24   25-34
   35-45   46-55   Over 55

9. How many hours per week do you read? _____

Name _____

Occupation _____

Address _____

City _____ State _____ Zip _____

...Hearts ♥ong...

..... Presents ....

Great Inspirational Romance at a Great Price!

Heartsong Presents books are inspirational romances in contemporary and historical settings, designed to give you an enjoyable, spirit-lifting reading experience. You can choose from 84 wonderfully written titles from some of today's best authors like Colleen L. Reece, Brenda Bancroft, Janelle Jamison, and many others.

When ordering quantities less than twelve, above titles are $2.95 each.

SEND TO: Heartsong Presents Reader's Service
P.O. Box 719, Uhrichsville, Ohio 44683

Please send me the items checked above. I am enclosing $_____
(please add $1.00 to cover postage per order. OH add 6.5% tax. PA and NJ add 6%.). Send check or money order, no cash or C.O.D.s, please.
To place a credit card order, call 1-800-847-8270.

NAME _____

ADDRESS _____

CITY/STATE_____ ZIP _____

HPS JULY
